Quickies – 4
A Black Lace erotic short-story collection

**Look out for our themed Wicked Words and Black Lace
short-story collections:**

Already Published: *Sex in the Office, Sex on Holiday,
Sex in Uniform, Sex in the Kitchen, Sex on the Move,
Sex and Music, Sex and Shopping, Sex in Public, Sex
with Strangers*

Published August 07: *Paranormal Erotica*
(short-stories and fantasies)

Quickies – 4
A Black Lace erotic short-story collection

Black Lace books contain sexual fantasies.
In real life, always practise safe sex.

This edition published in 2007 by
Black Lace
Thames Wharf Studios
Rainville Road
London W6 9HA

Tighthead	© Nuala Deuel
Second Skin	© Candy Wong
Going Down on the Blues	© Carmel Lockyer
Priceless	© Mathilde Madden
Confessions	© Primula Bond
Geek God	© Violet Parker

Typeset by SetSystems Limited, Saffron Walden, Essex

Printed and bound by Mackays of Chatham PLC

ISBN 978 0 352 34129 7

Tighthead Nuala Deuel

I've heard them all, all those so-called jokes. About how we like to play with odd-shaped balls. And what exactly does the hooker get up to during a match? I wouldn't mind mauling with you, love. Fancy a ruck? Don't get me started on the scrum down. The only thing I wondered about was that business regarding repressed homosexuality. All that testosterone buzzing around, slamming into each other: an eighty-minute bump and grind that would drop jaws all round if it were happening anywhere else but on a rugby pitch. I doubted I'd ever nail that particular rumour.

Especially as I'm a girl, the only woman in an all-male fifteen.

You might have read about me in the papers. There was a big froth from the sport's governing body when they found out and I was banned from turning out for my team, The Rope & Anchor, a pub outfit playing in a minor league, but rules is rules. The local press pricked up their ears and mounted a big campaign to let me play rugby again and the suits, under pressure from equal-rights campaigners and big names from the sport (I had my picture taken with, among others, Will Carling, Rob Andrew and Jeremy Guscott), stepped down. I was back in my hooped top and shorts, taping up my fingers and ears before matches on drizzly weekends, matching the guys pint for pint in the Rope afterwards. I loved my teammates and I loved the game. I didn't think anything could ruin things after that. But that was before Jamie Garland came to play for us.

It was Steamo, our captain, an uncompromising second-row monolith of a man, who brought Jamie along to training one night. And I knew I was done for. It wasn't because Jamie played in my position – he was a tighthead prop and I was blindside flanker – or that we took an instant dislike to each other that would have meant disrupting the harmony of our team: it was the opposite. The moment I saw him – his shorn head, the taut bulk of his shoulders, the solid meat of his thighs as they moved beneath the lycra shorts he was running in – I knew I would give anything to have him.

I avoided the showers and deflected the invitations to join the team for a post-training beer and decided to go home, a headache building behind my eyes. Headaches are what I get when I'm so high on desire that I think I'll pass out. It's been a long time since I've had to reach for the Nurofen. Being surrounded by a bunch of men seeping the subtle smell of hot seed from every pore is not necessarily the thrill you might think it to be. I treat these boys like my brothers, and they are as protective and supportive of me as if I were their kid sister. Sex doesn't come into it. I even shower with these bruisers; I soap their backs for them. The nearest I ever came to fancying one of them was Steamo himself, but he's so professional, so dedicated to his sport that I would have had to accompany him on five-mile runs three times a week to be in with a chance of ever sharing his bed. So no, if there were going to be any dressing room fuckathons with me at the bottom of a pile of sweating limbs, it would have happened by now, I can promise you.

But Jamie Garland . . .

I drifted for what seems like hours. I was like Sigourney Weaver in *The Year of Living Dangerously* in the scene where she leaves her room, in a trance it would seem, driven by her need to make love to Mel Gibson. I understood that impulse now as I meandered along the streets, feeling a fist of heat unclench in my belly, its fingers reaching out to touch me, drag slow fingers over my puckered breasts, test the heat building between my legs. If I'd known where Jamie lived . . . well, I don't know what I might have done. We hadn't exchanged more than two words: hello and goodbye.

I got home, poured myself a stiff drink and sipped it while I soaked away the mud and the aches in a hot, deep bath. I couldn't get the image of Jamie's legs from my mind or the curve of his iron buttocks as he burrowed into another practice scrum, his shoulders, the way they arched and rolled as he worked to gain purchase in the turf. There wasn't a shred of fat on his body.

The glass made a soft, clinking sound as I set it

down uncertainly on the side of the bath. I was too absorbed by my daydreams to care if I spilt any. Candlelight flickered and surged against the wall like the play of muscle in a body filled with drive and purpose. My heartbeat was sending out steady tremors through the water; my breath provided a rhythmic background. I always drew baths that were way too hot. I could feel sweat spiking my forehead but I didn't wipe it away; I liked the feeling of gathering tensions, minor discomforts. Grit shifted on the foot of the bathtub. It prickled my arse and I liked that too. Jamie's feet might have disturbed some of that soil.

I stretched in the bath and saw through satisfied, half-shut eyes the swells of my breasts break the surface of the water. I have smallish breasts – a good thing, really, if you're playing a high-contact sport like rugby – but my nipples tend to become erect very easily when I play so I usually cover them up with a few criss-crosses of black gaffer tape. This also helps to prevent any more smart mouthing from opposition players, especially on cold days. Now I traced my own fingers over those soft nubs and felt the twinge in my loins as my body answered a familiar call. I enclosed one breast with my palm and imagined Jamie's lips doing the same job, softly sucking my entire tit – almost inhaling it – into his mouth. My other hand strayed south. I felt my fingers reach my soft, unruly bush and bump against my clit.

Such a hard body, he had. I wondered what his

cock looked like. I reached further and felt the folds of my lips, the way they felt slightly more viscous than the water that sloshed around them. I arched my back and began to softly strum myself . . . and the telephone rang.

The moment passed. I was a slightly stocky girl again, sitting in a muddy bath, the hot smell of scotch rising from the towels on the floor. I pulled on my tatty bathrobe and picked up the phone in the hall. It was Steamo.

'What happened tonight?' he asked.

In the background I could hear his blender working full throttle: another batch of his renowned protein smoothies. He probably had a piece of fish steaming and a large plateful of iron-rich greens. He was a dedicated man where fitness was concerned.

'Nothing, why?' My voice carried a tweak of petulance about it.

Steamo wasn't stupid. He knew his players. Precious little slipped by the captain's attention and trying to bluff him wasn't going to wash, but it didn't stop me trying. I couldn't just bleat my feelings to him, not after one stupid, smitten evening. It was my problem. I had to get a grip of myself. I had to deal with it.

'You were playing like you'd tied your boots together.'

'We all have off days,' I said.

'Is there something you're hiding from me? About Jamie?'

Unusually perceptive, our captain. I caught my

reflection in the hallway mirror and snapped my mouth shut.

'Loz? Loz? You there?'

'I'm here,' I said.

'So? What is it? Do you know him or something? Have you two got some history?'

If only ... 'No. No. It's nothing to do with Jamie. I don't know why you even mention him.'

'Because you were staring at him half the night as if he was playing with a third leg. I mean it, Loz, if there's some back story you're not telling me about then –'

'There's nothing. I swear. I don't know the guy.' I bit my lip. 'Where's he from, anyway? What's *his* back story? I mean, where does he live?'

The blender cut out. There was silence at the end of the phone. And then, very quietly, with a tone in his voice that told me he was smiling, he said, 'You fancy him, that's it, isn't it?'

'Oh go to hell!' I slammed the phone down. How dare he? How dare he reduce what he saw as my failings on the training ground to some girly crush? I had half a mind to call him back and tell him to stick his team. And then I saw my reflection in the mirror again. I was smiling too.

We had a match that weekend away to Cherry Wood Lions, the league leaders. Steamo wanted us to convene at a pub in the town centre for a light pre-match lunch where he would run through a few tactics and plays that we might deploy during the game. I picked at my salad while the other boys tucked into their pasta. I watched the way Jamie ate and imagined his jaws moving like that as he tongued my sex. I squeezed my thighs together and forced myself to concentrate on what Steamo was saying.

When the plates had been cleared away Steamo clapped his hands together and said: 'Right, let's get on the road. Everyone know the way?'

I was driving Munny, our fly-half, and Goose, the full-back, down to the ground in my old Citroën. We were in the car park when Steamo called to me. 'Loz? Jamie's got a flat. Can you squeeze him in?'

I gabbled some affirmative reply while I hurried myself into the driving seat and prayed the blush away from my cheeks. Munny got into the back with Goose before I could ask one of them to sit up front with me. There was a forced smile on my lips as Jamie eased his monster frame into the seat beside mine.

'Tight fit,' he said.

'Oh yeah,' I replied lightly, feeling the heat come back to my face.

I don't remember the drive to the ground. I recall the smell of Jamie's skin and the dull pain building up in my head to a point where I thought I would either black out or crash the car. I dared not look at him while I steered. All I saw was his smooth strong right hand resting on the crease-free expanse of his right thigh. Clean fingernails, square cut. I could see that hand cupping me, rubbing me, becoming wet with my juices as I bucked and writhed against his fingers. I wanted that hand clamped over my mouth as I came. I wanted it turned hot with my breath and oaths. I wanted to be able to smell myself on it long hours later.

I parked the car and he got out. I had almost forgotten that Munny and Goose were in the back. We unloaded our sports bags and traipsed across gravel and grass to the Portakabins that were Cherry Wood Lions' dressing rooms. The pitch beyond them was pale with a thin wintry mist. There were maybe a dozen spectators spread out around the touchline and a couple of dogs. The sun was trying its best to make itself known through the high blanket of cloud but only a vague bright patch hinted at its location. The cold hung in the air like something that could be touched. I followed the others into the cabin, hoping I'd remembered to pack my tape.

I tried my best not to watch Jamie while he pulled on his shorts and shirt. Only the thought of Steamo's smug expression prevented me from glancing at Jamie's body, though I sorely wanted to. I allowed myself a brief glimpse as he was bent over his boots, tying his laces. I saw his muscles flexing in his arm and that was enough to be going on with. I taped up my boobs, hoping he might be watching me, and pulled on my number-six shirt.

The match itself was a scrappy affair, mired for the most part in midfield, where the recycled ball was never used to as good effect as it might. The kicking was awry, the tackles mistimed and there were an unusual number of knock-ons; it didn't help that the pitch started cutting up after twenty minutes. We went into half time 26–10 down. All of our points had been from converted penalties whereas the Cherries had scored two tries. It always bothered Steamo if we hadn't been able to impose ourselves try-wise. We decided at the break to run the ball more. If we were going to lose then at least we would do so in style.

'Quick hands,' Steamo said as we trotted back to our positions. 'Pass, move, support.'

Almost as soon as we won possession we scored a try, the ball fumbled by their full-back when a simple kick into touch seemed the likely outcome. It was Steamo himself, true to his name, powering through to block the clearance and dive for the line. The try converted, we were a changed outfit. We swung the ball left and right, the team's line unbending, unbroken, like something impelled by arcane mathematics. Ten minutes to go, the score 26–24 in their favour, I intercepted a pass and took off, my eyes fast on the posts. I'm quick when I get going and I could hear the laboured breathing of their backs as they tried to bring me down. One of them managed to trip me, a last-ditch tap of my foot that cause me to overbalance. Bodies piled in. I tried to keep possession without incurring a penalty and forced the ball back under my body, waiting for it to be recycled.

In the melee I felt a hand squirm under my top and squeeze my left breast. I jerked away, ready to unleash a great torrent of abuse, when I saw the square-cut fingernails of the hand that had groped me. The bodies were getting off. The referee was peering in, trying to make sense of the pile-up. I took hold of the hand before it disappeared and sucked the forefinger into my mouth, squirmed my tongue against it, gave it a little nip.

We scored another try, a scrappy push for the line, with a couple of minutes to go. The conversion was sliced wide of the posts but it didn't matter. We'd beaten the league leaders 26–29. The excitement of the win was enough to keep my mind off what had happened between me and Jamie. When I remembered, as I tugged my knickers free, I felt a jolt of electricity jag up through my pelvis as if his fingers had done the job for me. Naked, I brushed past him on my way to the showers. He was still in his shorts, trading bellows of triumph with Steamo and Goose, but he noticed the smear of my thigh against his arse. I know he did. I spent ten minutes longer in the shower than was necessary but he didn't appear out of the mist to stand under the spigot next to mine. Disgruntled I wrapped myself in towels and left, just as he was stepping by me. I smiled at him, desperate to look down at his cock, but I couldn't. Not until I was sure about him.

The boys were almost dressed. I took my time towelling my hair and then made a show of looking for my shampoo. Stomach churning, I headed back to the showers. He was still there, on his own. I stopped. It felt as though my tongue had grown too thick for my mouth. I looked around because I heard someone knocking on the door but it was me: it was my heart.

Oh God. He was standing under a jet of water, his hand wrapped around the shaft of his cock, and he was soaping himself slowly, thoroughly, and turning his head this way and that to watch how his prick shifted as he stroked. He didn't have a full erection, not yet, but his prick was swollen and heavy. It gleamed under the wet lights. I heard its soft sucking sounds and the light slap of his hand's edge as it bounced against his lathered balls. I reached inside the towel skirt I had fashioned and my fingers confirmed what I thought. I was sopping. I was ready for him. Was he waiting here for me?

But I couldn't go to him. Something was holding me back. Not just the arresting sight of him lazily tossing himself off, although deliciously that would have been reason enough. It was the fear that I had got it wrong, that it wasn't his hand that had squeezed my tit. It was the fear that Steamo would walk in on us and decide that inter-team fucking was not the best preparation for a league campaign.

I chewed my lip, began to edge away from the steam. There would be plenty of opportunities. There would be dozens of dressing rooms, showers and –

'Don't go.' He looked up at me, his hand still working himself, a thick tide of soap dripping from the head of his cock, his tight, swollen balls.

He asked me to wash his back.

I did so, all my fears evaporating, dissolving into the steam. I no longer cared who might stumble upon us. His skin was creamy and tight against the muscles beneath. Freckles were scattered across his back in random patterns, like constellations. I found myself studying them, as if trying to unpack their meaning. He turned towards me and said thank you. His face was filled with colour, his lips ruddy. He looked as though he was going to say something else but he simply turned his attention back to his dick. He was hard now. The flesh of his cock tight, his slit like a small mouth shaping an O of ecstasy.

'Your hand must be getting tired,' I said, my voice thick in my throat.

He didn't say anything but released his grip. His prick swung lazily upright and bobbed at me as I reached out for him.

'Do you want me to help you with that tape?' he asked. His soft, brown eyes never blinked. They were staring hard into mine, searching me, testing my limit. The only way I could have given him more encouragement would have been if my eyes were green. I focused on his cock and nodded, unable to speak. I thought that if I opened my mouth I might scream.

I held him and even under the heat of the water powering from the shower his heat was greater. I felt the soft outer sheath of his dick move against its rock-hard core. I ran my thumb over the glistening tip and wondered how he would taste, how he could fill every vacuum in my body. His fingers teased back the shiny black crosses of tape and I heard his breath turn ragged, whether at the pressure I was exerting with my fingers or the sight of my breasts I'm not sure. I'd like to think it was down to a little of both. He leant over and ran his tongue over my nipples. Water crashed against the back of his neck, making his shoulders gleam. I wanted to say something, wanted to warn him that someone might come in, but none of that mattered. I pressed him back against the wall and the torrent disfigured his face: all I could tell was that his eyes were shut and his mouth open.

I sank to my knees and let the moment spin out before me, his cock twitching above me now, my fingers at its base, gently pressing against his balls, peeling his foreskin back to reveal his sensitive inner, making him sleek and long. I paused with my mouth a millimetre away from it, needles of hot water pricking me all over my face. I dabbed at him with my tongue then, unable to wait any longer, let his entire length slide between my lips until my nose mashed against his pubes. I sucked at him greedily, loving the feel of his steely thighs under my fingers and the dense, filling sensation of his cock in my mouth. I kneaded at his buttocks, wanting him to come in my mouth, but he gently pushed me away and whispered that he wanted to fuck. The drumming of the water, the thrum of pain in my head, matched with the pulse of desire between my legs

– if he didn't fill me up there I was going to have to rub myself – it was all becoming too much. I thought I might faint.

I turned around and pressed the side of my face against the floor, presented myself to him, slipped my forearms through the inverted V created by my legs and gently teased apart the sodden lips of my sex. Not the most ladylike of offerings, I know, but I'm a rugby player. I know what I want and how to get it. I wanted him to pound me into the ground. I wanted him deep.

I felt the head of his cock widen me as he pushed in. Then slowly, deliriously, he began pumping and I could feel every wonderful inch of him as my pussy drew him in. I touched myself and felt him too, where our bodies were joined, where a perfect seal was formed. His balls drummed against me. I felt a soapy finger stroke the super-sensitive flesh of my anus. Suds and water sluiced around my face and I felt the textured tiles beneath me scrape my nipples as I jiggled against them. The slap of his hard stomach against my arse. It was all too much. Building, it was building within so intensely I thought I would burst. I felt the first powerful surge of an orgasm plough through me and as I began to moan felt him increase his pace. I came again and ground myself against him. His hands grabbed hold of me roughly by the hips. I was vaguely aware of a presence at the shower entrance watching us through the clouds of steam but by then I didn't care. I let myself be fucked as though it were the last time for both of us. I felt him begin to tense and, although I wanted to feel him spray all that heat inside me, I wanted to see it happen even more. I wriggled off him and turned around, and I got hold of his cock just as he was beginning to come. I guided the head of his prick against my chest and felt his impossibly hot spunk draw a glorious route across the map of my body. Jamie's face was nothing but the clenched bar of his teeth and tightly screwed eyes. I kneaded his balls as another jet of come sizzled out of him, whipping across my cheek. I coaxed another few drops from him and then, spent, he came back to the real world. The person at the entrance was gone.

I leant over and kissed the tip of his cock clean as he dwindled. He tasted fresh and spicy, like the marine tang of the sea. Neither of us could say much. We showered, soaping each other clean, then meekly tiptoed back to the changing rooms. Happily, the other players had decamped to the bar. We dressed quickly and, before leaving, he pulled me close. 'I haven't even kissed you yet,' he said.

We both laughed, embarrassed by the strength of our carnality. I kissed him now, pressing my body fully against his, and broke away when things started to get too heated again.

'Come home with me tonight?' he said.

'Yes,' I said. I felt I could go through my whole life with him and say no other word. 'Steamo's not going to be happy about this,' I said. 'I mean, it isn't good form to have your tighthead and your flanker getting up close and personal, is it?'

'Steamo can go and drop-kick himself through the posts for all I care,' Jamie said.

'He could have done that to me too, after what you did to me out on that pitch. I wouldn't have noticed.'

Jamie's expression faltered. 'What do you mean?'

I punched his arm gently. 'You know exactly what I mean. When you copped a feel of my puppies.'

He blinked and the smile died from his face.

'Oh dear,' I said. 'That wasn't you?'

He shook his head.

In the bar we got a few suspicious glances from the other players, but nobody said anything. Neither of us could enjoy those drinks, despite what had happened in the changing rooms. We inspected the faces of our opponents, wondering which one of them could have committed such an odious act. I felt like going to each one in turn and shaking them by the hand, just so I could inspect their fingernails.

'Forget it,' Jamie said, and winked at me. 'I'll buy you dinner.'

'We're not leaving together, are we?'

'Of course. You gave me a lift, didn't you? I'll need a lift back.'

Goose and Munny came too, which saved us from being grist for the gossip mill, and I contrived a route that meant they would have to get out of the car first. When we were alone again, I asked Jamie what he wanted to eat.

'You,' he said. 'In the back of the car.'

I laughed, but his hand was already worming its way between my legs. I shifted in my seat, feeling hot colour bloom on my cheeks for the second time in as many hours.

'Jamie,' I started to protest but, even as I said his name, I was clambering into the back seat, only pausing to hitch up my skirt and hook a finger in my gusset to draw it to one side, 'we're on a main road.'

'Don't worry,' he said. 'It's too late in the day to get a parking ticket.'

And then he dropped his head between my legs and I felt his tongue and lips probing me. I could feel my juices and his saliva dribbling down the soft skin of my inner thigh. The car filled with the smell of my sex and the windows misted over. He kissed and sucked my clit while he drove the tips of his fingers under my bra, cupped and stroked my breasts with a pleasing roughness that stayed just the right side of pain.

I lifted my legs and planted the soles of my feet on the ceiling of the car. I felt his tongue lick around my anus and I gasped when he jabbed it in, his other finger now alternating between rubbing my mons and exploring my creases. I came suddenly, with a force that twisted my knee and caused me to almost put my foot through the window.

I wanted to return the favour but a police car

had parked across the road from us. We surreptitiously straightened our clothes and I tidied up my hair in the rear-view mirror. My knee had flared up quite badly by now but I didn't give it much thought. Before pulling away from the kerb I leant over and licked away the drying juices on his chin and cheeks.

We got back to his place and he cooked dinner. Then we went to bed and I didn't get any sleep until the colour of the night was draining away from the rooftops. I was going to have to buy a family pack of headache tablets after all this.

We had training the following evening, a light session of stretching and swimming, to help our bodies repair after the rigours of the match. I should have cried off; my knee was quite badly swollen, but I didn't want to give Steamo any more ammunition to have a go at me. I could tell something wasn't quite right when I started a series of stretches to benefit the thigh muscles. I heard something pop and greyed out for a while. When I came to, Jamie was leaning over me. I looked down. A cold compress was positioned over my knee.

'Ouch,' I said.

'Looks like you've bust your cruciates from where I'm standing,' he said.

'What's that mean in English?'

'No more rugby,' Steamo said. He sat down by my side. 'Sorry, kiddo. You've had it.'

He reached out and patted my hand. The shock of the moment seemed too great. It was only a game. A game I loved but, still, it wasn't the be all and end all of my life. And then I realised why my shock felt so profound. Steamo's fingernails were clean and square cut.

So I left the team. The injury put paid to my rugby future, but I would have turned my back on them anyway, after what our skipper had done to me that day. I was furious. Jamie was ample compensation, however, and I let him know how much I appreciated him every night, to the point where we were both collecting bags under our eyes and I was beginning to get saddle sore.

Then, one night, there was a knock at the door.

'Leave it,' I said. We'd just uncorked the wine and sat down to eat. I didn't want any distractions.

He got up, a trifle sheepishly. 'I can't,' he said. 'I invited him.'

'Who?' But, as I asked the question, I knew exactly. 'Jamie!'

To his credit, Steamo was very contrite. He had bought me a bottle of wine to aid the apology and said it was totally out of character, which was true enough, I suppose. And he was man enough to admit, in front of Jamie, that the only reason he did it was out of desperation: he was jealous of my obvious attraction to the new boy which had forced his hand.

'It was stupid of me. Ill thought out. But, I hope, not unforgivable.'

'Oh, come here, you,' I said, and hugged him. I glimpsed Jamie licking his lips.

'I saw you in the shower,' Steamo said. 'I was

coming in after you ... I thought you'd given me the come-on when you, you know, sucked my finger out on the pitch. I just got the wrong end of the stick.'

Jamie's eyes were glittering. I couldn't believe what I was seeing. He was getting off on me hugging Steamo, my tiny hands flat against his powerful back. I have to admit, Steamo's mouth was very close to my throat and the vibration of his words gave me a little tickle. I held him for longer than seemed correct.

'I used to fancy you,' I said. 'But you were too high maintenance. I wouldn't have been able to keep up with you.'

'Pity,' Steamo said. 'I think we could have been great together. You've got a beautiful body.'

'So have you,' I said. My heart was thudding so hard I thought Steamo might get a bruised chest.

'Me and Jamie,' Steamo said, 'we go way back.'

'Yeah,' Jamie said, unfastening the top button of his shirt. 'We share everything.'

I pushed Steamo away and smiled. I was too thrilled by what was happening to be angry. But I wasn't going to let them get their own way so easily. It was time to find out, once and for all.

'Remember, I've got a dodgy knee, boys,' I said. 'But I'll think about letting you share me ... if you share each other first.'

Nuala Deuel is the co-author of *Princess Spider: True Experiences of a Dominatrix*, and has had short fiction published in numerous Wicked Words collections.

Second Skin Candy Wong

It was a late spring day in Paris, and I found myself in the happy position of having nothing particular to do. I strolled around the Marais district for a while, looking at all the chic little boutiques with their cooler-than-thou staff smoking in the doorways, but nothing snagged my interest. After browsing *Pariscope* over a late-morning croissant and a *grand crème*, I set off for the Champs-Elysées.

It took a while to find a film I liked the sound of. I was in a funny, aimless, mood, you see – not bored, exactly, but unable to invest in anything that didn't grasp me fully. And I wasn't at all sure what that something might be. All up the strip leading to the Arc de Triomphe, signboards shrieked out the names of the latest blockbuster offerings, and from huge posters Hollywood's darlings smiled down, teeth flashing an unnatural white.

Eventually, senses dulled by the roar of the traffic and dazzle of the April sunshine, I took a side street more or less at random, and before long I found myself outside a small two-screen picture house, staring at a poster of a young woman, barely clad and with hair dishevelled, sitting astride a wooden bench looking up at a much older, fully clothed man. In the background, canvases were ranged against a stone wall. An artist's studio, and she his model, I thought. *Research*. I had found some point to my day, a focus. I stepped inside, hand already clasped around my purse in my pocket.

Behind smoky glass, an elderly woman with frothy henna-red hair and matching fingernails sat thumbing through a gossip magazine. She looked up as the door closed behind me, and gave me a look that managed to be both slightly startled and bored at the same time.

'What time's the next showing?' I asked, gesturing towards a second poster on the wall by her kiosk. This time the young woman had her bare back and shoulder to the man, but her head was half-turned to him, and her expression was one of distrust, perhaps even accusation. His hand hovered at her rounded brown shoulder.

Her eyes followed my gaze. '*La Belle Noiseuse?* Half an hour.'

'Who's the actress?' I said, pulling a hundred-franc note from my purse and handing it to her.

'Béart. Emmanuelle Béart. You know – the chick who was in *Manon des Sources*.'

I hadn't seen it, but the girl did look familiar, with her wide, childlike eyes, her impressive pout. She looked like the type who got her own way every time, simply by putting her hands on her hips, pushing out those lips and looking for all the

world as if one almighty tantrum was about to be
unleashed.

'Can I go in early?' I asked as the woman
handed me my change and a ticket.

'Sure.' She waved me towards a door to the
right of the kiosk. I hadn't brought a book with
me, unable, as I left my little rented *chambre de
bonne* that morning, to decide what I fancied. I
spotted a pile of promotional film magazines on a
little ledge by the doorway, though, and filched
one on my way in. It would pass the time.

Ten minutes later, alone in the screening room,
I had learned that '*la belle noiseuse*' meant 'the
beautiful troublemaker', and referred to a seven-
teenth-century prostitute that the artist in the
film was trying to paint, using his wife as a model.
He becomes blocked, but when he meets the character played by Béart he finally returns to the
canvas. The obvious complications ensue.

I studied the pictures of Béart again, and then I
put the magazine aside, stifling a yawn. I'd also
learned from the article that the full-length version was more than three hours long. I checked
my ticket: this was that version. This had better
light my fire, I thought, or I'm out of here.

The door creaked open behind me, and I turned
to see who my fellow viewer or viewers might be.
With the sun flooding in from behind, however, I
could only make out a woman's silhouette: the
line of a skirt, slightly flared at the bottom; a mass
of curls sparking in the light; headgear of some

kind. I looked at the screen, then cocked my head so that I could observe her move down the walkway from out of the corner of my eye, without obviously staring over my shoulder at her.

The lights dimmed as I did so, and the curtains parted, slowly, with a certain sense of drama. I wondered if they still did that in the multiplexes, and couldn't remember having seen it of late. It seemed like a relic of a more elegant age, when going to the cinema was an occasion and not an excuse to fill one's belly with buckets of popcorn while leering at the latest idol.

My attention was taken by the screen now, and with the anticipation of the film to come, but through it I became aware that the woman's footsteps had come to a halt. I risked a glance to my right, and saw that she had stopped level with the row on which I was seated, halfway down the auditorium. She was looking at the screen. I stared back at it. The credits began to roll. I looked at the woman again and she was gone. The film began.

Béart, from the start, was mesmerising. I was in my mid-twenties by this time, and didn't think I was gay. But when I saw a woman with a body like that, I didn't understand why not. Through her pretty, strappy little sundress, the actress was fleshy, pulpy, her limbs the consistency of new dough just waiting, *asking* to be kneaded. Involuntarily, I saw after a while, my hands were caressing my thighs.

For the next half-hour, I was entranced, drawn into the film by Béart's physical presence: the way she walked, the colour and texture of her, those eyes. Then I became aware of another presence, and sure enough, up the row, I saw that the woman had returned and was watching again. This time, there was a bright outdoor scene on the screen and, in the ambient light, I could see her more clearly: the sheen of something pink, close fitting all over but especially clingy over her breasts and thighs, with wide lapels; spidery eyelashes and a button nose; and more pink in the form of a comical little pillbox hat, sitting slightly crooked on her mass of white-blonde candyfloss hair. In her left hand, I noticed, she clutched a slender black torch. I stifled a giggle. An usherette, I thought, how very old-fashioned. And more to the point: an usherette with nobody to usher. The one person who'd showed up had come in early and done her out of a job. Still, as long as she was getting paid, it wasn't as if she was going to complain.

I turned back to the screen, but this time it was harder to lose myself in the story. I guess the usherette's positioning of herself at the end of my row unnerved me, although there was nothing to indicate that she was even aware of me. But then, if there had been no one in the auditorium, why would she be here, and why would they even be showing the film at all? Every few minutes, I glanced back at her, convinced that this time I'd catch her watching me, but each time she'd still be looking at the screen, face expressionless. She'd probably seen the film countless times, knew every scene and every word of dialogue. Yet here she was, watching again. What was she waiting for?

The stakes were rising in the film: Béart is livid that her husband has 'sold her ass' by promising the painter she will model for him. Secretly, though, she is flattered, and fascinated, and before her husband rises the next morning, she sneaks out to the artist's château and they go to his studio, where she begins to pose for him. It's only a matter of time before, as if by some unspoken agreement between the artist and his model, she takes off all her clothes.

Béart, as I've already said, is not skinny. She has that kind of voluptuousness that makes you feel – or made me feel – as if you can reach out into the screen and touch her. And that moment when she steps towards the painter and shrugs off her robe – well, let's just say, I don't think there's anyone, man or woman, who could hand on heart say it doesn't send a little shiver up through them.

Something – a weird feeling – made me turn my head to the right, and the usherette was now looking at me. Or rather, I couldn't make out her eyes in the dim light from the screen, but her face was definitely turned in my direction. Then slowly, not at all guiltily or self-consciously, she moved it back towards the screen.

I did the same, but I sensed an old familiar itch mounting in my groin, a sudden wetness in my panties. Only now I wasn't convinced that this time it was Béart who was tugging my strings.

Try as I might to concentrate on the film, and despite the actress's lush magnificence, it was all I could do to keep myself from turning back to the usherette. At the limits of my vision I could sense her there, just a few steps away from me, and something told me she was getting as heated up as I was. When finally I could take it no more, I turned my head towards her and, sure enough, she was writhing in her seat, her body moving rhythmically like that of a snake being charmed out of its basket. I pulled myself up in mine to get a better look, and saw that she had unbuttoned her dress at the hips and inserted one hand, with which she was unmistakably working at herself. My hand moved to my crotch of its own accord, began mimicking her actions. Separated by only a few feet, we advanced towards our separate climaxes.

And then suddenly, with no warning, she was there at my side, dress still flapping open at the middle, eyes blazing down at me, a half-smile on her lips. I stared up at her, half appalled, half thrilled by her brazenness, but there must have been an invitation or at least consent in my eyes because all at once she had swung her leg over and was astride me, one knee balanced on each arm of my seat. One hand clutched the back of the seat, while with the other she undid the lower buttons of her dress, from her knee to her thigh. My breath felt harsh in my throat, constricted by a mixture of blind lust and panic, but once it had begun to come more easily again, I reached up, tentatively, and pulled aside the black lace of her knickers to reveal her tidy little pussy, blonde and pruned. With the other hand, I stroked the satin of her inner thigh. Her bush, wispy as a baby's hair, brushed the back of my fingers. My hand spasmed. I felt clumsy, gauche.

I reached up for her breasts, still concealed beneath the sheer fabric. My hands hesitated on the pearlescent buttons, but any last shred of doubt was blown away when I pulled open the top part of her dress and reached inside for her. She was wearing a black balcony bra that pushed her breasts upwards and forwards, as if serving them up on a plate. 'Here they are!' it seemed to say. I reached round her with one hand and untethered them. They sprang forth, warm and perky, the areolae as hard as nuts under my fingertips yet strangely compliant, as if beckoning me into the darkness of her uniform.

I brought my face up to her, buried my face in the shadows, and jabbed at her right nipple with my tongue, then circled it over and over again. My tongue flicked at her like a flame in a draught. She moaned softly once or twice, but when I looked up at her face I found that she was watching the screen. I directed my own gaze towards it and watched as Béart strode across the artist's studio, a provocative look in her eyes, that famous pout out in full force.

I backed off, lowered my hands to her pussy again, brandishing them rather ineffectually in the region of her clitoris. I felt like a novice, an amateur. I was boring her.

'Come on, come *on*,' she said, urgently, the first words that I ever heard her utter, and I held my breath, bunched my fingers together and delved into her wet core. Her hips began to gyrate, and inside I felt her muscles clench around me, as if trying to suck me further inside her. She let out a wail, as if she was losing all control of herself, and then, with a shudder that ran through her whole body, she threw back her head and I watched, electrified, as her face, caught in the light streaming down into the room from the projector, contorted, illuminated in its ecstasy.

I didn't see her on my way out. She had left quickly, not looking back as she picked up her torch from the seat at the end of the row and strode out of the auditorium. The remainder of the film went over my head as I replayed the strange encounter over and over in my mind, all the time wondering if I'd dozed off and dreamed it. Part of me wanted to leave at once, of course; to go and find the gorgeous blonde creature and talk about what had happened between us. But part of me was afraid: afraid that in the light of day she would shun me, deny what had happened, laugh at me.

I needn't have worried, since there was no sign of her when I left the cinema and walked back out into the cold, hard sunlight. I thought of waiting around for her to finish her shift, assuming she hadn't already, but again, the fear of rejection or ridicule dissuaded me from hanging about. It had been a moment of madness, I told myself, and both of us would be better off forgetting it as quickly as possible.

I finished my art history degree a few weeks afterwards and, unsure of what I wanted to do with the rest of my life, spent a few months travelling, having adventures along the way, with both men and women. It was as if the experience with the usherette had unleashed some new potential in me, the freedom to finally become who I had been all along, if only I had been brave enough to see it rather than conforming to other people's expectations. Or thinking that I had to be one way or the other, without compromise. After a while, though, all the faces, all the anonymous bodies of both sexes, began to blur into one, and behind them all I saw only the flushed face of the usherette, haloed by dust motes, caught in its rapture in the beam from above. I realised then that I had run away from Paris, and from my need to see her again.

I made it as far as the door of the cinema several times but never dared venture in. Then, one day, I saw that they were showing *La Belle Noiseuse* again, for just one week, and I knew that fate was calling out to me. I went inside and handed over another ten-franc note to the same flame-haired ticket woman, feeling as if time had stood still. Heart racing, I pushed open the door to the auditorium.

The usherette was in there already, her back to me. Her sheer uniform gleamed in the half light, so tight around her buttocks it was almost a part of her. As before, her hair was pinned up loosely under her jaunty little hat, and I had a moment to admire the shape of her neck before she slowly turned around and regarded me without the least trace of surprise.

'Where would you like to sit?' she said with that same half-smile that she had worn when she had appeared at my side with her dress gaping open, beckoning me into her folds.

I was so taken aback by her coolness that I could barely reply. 'Er – I – I really don't mind.'

She swept her torch over the room. 'As you can see,' she said, 'you have the run of the place.'

'It's not a very popular film,' I observed.

'Not in the daytime, it's true,' she replied. 'This first showing is quiet for everything, though. It's not really worth anyone's while, but my boss insists.' She shrugged. 'He's an old-fashioned, romantic type of guy. No commercial sense at all.'

I had been trailing her down the auditorium, and now, as I followed the train of her torch beam, I saw that she was directing me to the very same seat that I had occupied before. 'Thank you,' I spluttered as I made my way down the row, unsure whether to laugh or to turn on my heels. I was afraid she was making fun of me, playing a game with me.

'*My* pleasure,' I heard her call as she walked back up towards the door. I winced.

The film began, but this time I had no eyes for Béart, and instead spent an uncomfortable half-hour gazing unseeingly at the screen while straining my ears for any sound from the usherette. I felt ridiculous, and imagined her back out at the kiosk, smoking a cigarette and sniggering about me with the old lady selling tickets. I had just convinced myself that it was time to leave when I heard the swish of satin against the seat beside me and looked up in time to see her lowering herself into it.

She looked at me with an unfathomable expression, left eyebrow raised; she seemed half mocking, half expectant. Then she slipped off her pillbox hat and bent her head towards me. She smelled of apples, and rain. I took hold of her head. 'Do you remember me?' I exhaled into the yellow explosion of her hair, and I held my breath, afraid of the answer.

'Of course,' she whispered back and, taking my face between her hands, she kissed me. 'You don't think I make a habit of this, do you?'

'I hope not –' I began, but already she had placed a finger on my lips to silence me.

'I've been waiting for you,' she said, and with her free hand she began plucking at the buttons on the lower half of her dress. I watched, powerless to act, in thrall to the way she decided what she wanted and went for it, unable to believe my luck that what she wanted was me. She half turned in her seat and lay back against the arm, legs agape. For a moment, pussy exposed to me, she stayed still, as if lost in thought. I inhaled the sweet-sour tang of her sex, observed the glisten and froth of her labia, like some creature sparkling in a sun-flooded rock pool. Then she appeared to come back to life and, wriggling her panties down over her thighs, flipped over, draped herself over the arm of her seat and presented herself to me.

I came to my senses then, and marvelled at the velvet of her cheeks as I parted her deep cleft with my hands and brought my face to her, dabbing at her sphincter with my tongue. It was perfectly pink and fragrant, like a tight little rosebud withholding its secrets, the flower it would become. She arced like a fish as I did so, gasping into the darkness, and then I saw her reach her hand down between her legs and within a few moments she climaxed beneath me, with a cry like shattered glass. And indeed, as if broken into pieces, she slumped back over the arm of the chair and remained motionless.

Unsated, desperate to prolong the experience, I yanked down my jeans and knickers and began massaging my clitoris vigorously. She sat up beside me now, leaned forwards, and without any need to wet me, inserted the handle of her little rubber torch into myself and began thrusting it in and out, her face searching mine for approval.

I nodded, feeling a warm friction against my walls.

'Harder?' she said.

'Harder. Please.'

'Like this?'

'*Harder.*'

I came as violently as she had, and then I lay breathless across her lap, watching the figures move across the screen but unable to make sense of their words or actions. Finally, I sat up and looked at the usherette in the semidarkness. She leaned forwards and scraped one hand about on the floor for her panties, her dress open to me, her hair falling about her face like a cloud of bright insects. Inside her dress I could see the nut brown of her nipples as she swayed to and fro.

'Can I see you naked?' I asked. Suddenly it felt strange to have been so intimate without getting undressed.

'This *is* me,' she said, as if precluding further discussion; her tone was curt, but I thought I caught an undertow of wistfulness in her words. And sure enough, in the silvery light from the screen, I saw that all the various pinks of her breasts, her sex, her uniform merged into one silken swatch, and I realised that the uniform was another skin to her.

We saw each other for a couple of months after that, but never at her place. We usually fucked at the cinema, at the early-afternoon showings whenever no one else showed up. I think the old lady in the kiosk must have guessed, but didn't much care, so long as we didn't leave stains. I

suppose she'd seen it all in all her years there –
forty-odd, according to Sylvie.

Sylvie, it turned out, was the usherette's name.
My girlfriend's name. It still seems weird saying
that, when she never did let me see her fully
unclothed, not even on the rare occasions when I
managed to lure her back to my attic room and
she had no excuse not to strip off. But I let it go,
after a while: she was so adventurous in other
ways, it wasn't worth arguing the toss about. One
night, for instance, she took me to Pigalle to sit in
a café and watch the prostitutes parading past the
window in their threadbare furs, then we went to
a cinema showing 1970s porn and played with
each other on the back row, behind all the old
men in their flasher macs thinking the main
action was on the screen. That was her idea of a
night out, as a couple.

The uniform was a constant, since, whenever
we met, Sylvie claimed she was either on her way
to or from work. I suspected she must have several
identical little pink dresses, because it never
looked grubby or crumpled, despite all the rough
and tumble it saw. In fact, it was the uniform that
alerted me to the fact that something was wrong.
We hadn't seen each other for a few days, and
then Sylvie hadn't shown up to a date we'd made
in a bar, and I went to the cinema off the Champs-
Elysées to see if she was still there. As soon as I
walked in I saw the pink dress hanging there, in
the little cloakroom beside the kiosk.

'Is Sylvie around?' I asked, though I already knew the answer.

'She left, a couple of days ago,' said the old lady, smacking her lips around a piece of gum, eyes already straying back to her magazine.

'Did she say anything?'

'Not much, just that she was looking for something new.'

I looked at the uniform, hanging faded and shapeless on a hanger like a sloughed-off skin, and then I turned and walked out into the Paris night, into the glare of neon and car lights. I wasn't sad. I had a feeling I would see Sylvie again. I just hoped I would recognise her in her latest disguise.

Candy Wong's short stories have appeared in numerous Wicked Words collections. She also writes as Carrie Williams and her first novel, *The Blue Guide*, is published by Black Lace in August 2007.

Going Down on the Blues
Carmel Lockyer

I've always been a wham-bam kind of girl. Or just a Wham kind of girl, if you want – George Michael could always do it for me, whether before, during or after we all found out that he likes boys. Well, I like boys too. But one day I woke up and realised the boys were all men, and 'Wake Me Up Before You Go-Go' didn't mean so much when you were 29 and you had to get up, make the bed, go to work, pay the mortgage, come home, get dolled up and go and find somebody else to mess up your bed for the night.

I talked to Jason about it. Jason was probably as big a Wham fan as I was – although he was also a big Duran Duran, Boy George and Steve Strange supporter. He was into that ruffled shirt and male mascara stuff when we were at school together, before the terms fag hag, gender bender and civil partnership were ever invented. But even Jason had found himself a live-in lover – by the name of Cedric – while I was still pretending 'Freedom' was my big thing.

'Chrissy, love,' Jason said, 'you've got to move

with the times. You know, play it a little cooler, a little slower.'

I blinked at him, then topped up my margarita from the pitcher and turned to Cedric. 'Do you know what he's talking about, Ceddie?'

'I think what the man was sayin' was that you're comin' on like the Material Girl and that's what the guys are pickin' up on – but what you're lookin' for is somebody you can rely on, yeah?'

'Cedric, you're drunk!' Jason took the plastic tumbler out of Ceddie's hand and pushed him towards the kitchen. 'Go and make us some nibbles while I introduce Chrissy to the world of the blues . . .'

Cedric vanished in a haze of alcohol and Jason leant towards me.

'Chrissy darling, I've known you since you were eight years old – trust me when I tell you that as long as you move to a disco beat, your men are going to last as long as a summer hit – if you want staying power, you've got to start thinking about what works in the long-player market.'

So I went home in a taxi with half a dozen of Jason's CDs and woke up with a stinking headache. It was Saturday, thank God, so I just brushed my teeth and sat on the sofa with a cushion on my lap to listen.

First up: Billie Holiday. I listened to three tracks, went into the kitchen and made a big pot of coffee, poured a slug of brandy into my mug and then headed to the bedroom. I pulled on my old black coat with the fun fur collar, a black lace teddy and a pair of high-heeled red suede stilettos, then I went back to sit on the sofa again, with my brandy coffee, and crossed my legs, letting a lot of thigh show in the gap between the sides of my the coat. Billie sang, 'Ain't Nobody's Business If I Do' and I sang along, gazing at myself in the mirror over the fireplace. This was cool, this was slow, this was ... sexy! By the time Billie got around to 'All the Way' I was feeling the need to go all the way myself.

About six months ago, I'd picked up this guy in a bar who actually had a little leather case in his car, full of the kinds of gadgets that men just love. On a first date I was never inclined to give a man the chance to express himself through technology, because you can never tell when an unknown lover is going to move from playing the fandango with a rabbit vibrator to playing hunt the disarticulated female corpse with a circular saw, but on this one occasion I had gone as far as toying with a glass dildo because it was so pretty. When we were kids, Jason and me, we'd played marbles, and this glass shaft was like a grown-up fantasy: marbles for lovers. It was swirled with amber and gold patterns like phoenix feathers, and when the guy showed me how well it warmed up, by dipping it in a bowl of hot water – well, I'd kind of taken to the glass bauble, more than I had to its owner, although he was gentleman enough to leave it behind in the morning.

Glass wasn't like plastic – I didn't have to think about my little gizmo rolling off some filthy conveyor belt somewhere in Taiwan; instead I could imagine a dark-eyed Hungarian gypsy pursing his lips and blowing into a ball of molten glass, shaping it and teasing it out and curling it into just the right shape, smiling all the time as he hand-made the perfect phallus just for me. That was one fantasy, anyway. Today though, I oiled my glass love charm with pure almond oil and just slid the tip inside me. Then I took a big mouthful of smooth coffee, feeling the hit of the brandy on my empty stomach, and lay down across the sofa so my head hung off the front with the fur collar of my coat framing my face and my legs were stretched up the back of the cushions. I was looking pretty flushed and rosy, I thought, as I watched myself in the mirror. I bent one leg to allow me to slide the dildo a little deeper, and then let the music wash over me while I twisted it gently in place so I could feel it warming inside me. Slow, the blues were all about slow. I bent the other leg, letting the stiletto heels hook into the top of the sofa and slid one hand inside my coat, pushing the strap of my teddy off my shoulder so that my left breast slid out of the lace and the nipple just peeked out from under the fur. I licked my finger and ran it around the areola, which tightened. I looked in the mirror – I thought I appeared extremely decadent, not a kiss-me-quick Wham kind of girl at all. I slid the dildo a little further into me, feeling the pleasure of the smooth surface. I let my left hand pinch and twist my nipple as my right hand began to pump the glass shaft in and out. Then I slipped my left hand inside the coat to sneak its way down to stroke my clitoris. Billie sang and I came – slowly.

It was a good start to the day and things could only get better.

I packed everything pink and sparkly that I owned into a box and slid it under the bed. I threw my fake tan and anklets in the bin and dug out my old suspender belt and a couple of pairs of black stockings. I parted my hair on one side and slicked it down with gel. I looked in the mirror: slow, cool and gorgeous, I thought.

That night I went to the Blues Garden in Camden – there was a jazz/blues band playing, called the Symposium. I felt really out of place, even in my black on black outfit and my new cool but sexy persona. I couldn't even think of anything to drink when I got to the bar. Normally I'd have whatever was blue, or pink, or came with an umbrella in it, or a two for the price of one offer on it, but suddenly that didn't sound cool enough.

'Bourbon,' I said, eventually. Billie had sung about it, so I would drink it. The barman lifted his eyebrow but poured the drink. It tasted like cat pee, to be honest.

I turned round to look at the band, bending my knee and letting my foot in its high black heel rest against the bar behind me. I was showing less cleavage than I'd displayed at any time since I got my first training bra, but an observant man would be able to spot the telltale shape on my raised thigh that showed a suspender belt concealed beneath the simple black dress. If there were any observant men – I noticed that although the crowd was better dressed than the one I usually mixed with on a Saturday night, it was also mainly couples, and the few men who were solo were gazing intently at the musicians rather than at me. Then I saw him – the Blues Brother of my dreams. Imagine Robert Redford dressed like Jools Holland, smiling like George Clooney and talking like Michael Caine – and you're not even close to Paul Gilcoyne. He played the saxophone, and stepped forwards to introduce each song. Why wasn't this bar packed with women straining to get at him? I asked myself for about ten seconds. Then I ran to the ladies', touched up my lippy, hauled on my bra straps to bring my cleavage right up under my chin and hitched up the skirt of my dress to flash a little flesh above the stocking. But I remembered what Jason had said: 'a little cooler, a little slower'. I left the lippy as it was, but lowered my bust to a less prominent angle and shimmied the skirt back down to its proper length. I walked back to my place at the bar slowly, very slowly, and stood with my back to the band. Within a minute Paul made eye contact with me in the mirror behind the bar, and I turned slowly, very slowly, and lifted my glass to him as he raised his glowing saxophone to me.

There's something incredibly sexy about a man who plays sax – think of Bill Clinton, for example. A man who's prepared to spend so much time getting his lips and tongue in exactly the right places, well ... a girl is going to recognise that as dedication to a good cause, isn't she? So as Paul serenaded me with his golden horn, I sipped the cat-piss drink and reminded myself I didn't have to grab my opportunities, I could simply wait for them to come to me.

An hour later we were in an alley outside the bar. I could feel the cold bricks against my spine and Paul warm against my front, as he whispered in my ear, 'Chrissy, what a beautiful name.'

I wanted to skim my skirt up so he could get his fingers inside me, but even if we managed to get that far, we'd never get any further because we'd have to negotiate the long buttoned flap of his coat, his shirt, his trousers ... bloody hell, this cool and slow stuff could be a nuisance at times. I could tell, though, that he was going to be worth waiting for – he was so focused and deliberate and he had a quirky little half-smile that lifted one corner of his mouth whenever he made me gasp or sigh, which he was doing fairly frequently. Long warm fingers too, which had managed to find their way swiftly inside the scoop neck of the dress, and were now tickling the back of my neck. They then moved down slowly but confidently to circle my breasts. He dragged his nails slowly across my ribs and made me shudder with desire, before sliding down again to grab my haunches and pull me into him. I pushed my shoulders against the wall and thrust my hips forwards. I lifted one leg to wrap around his arse and pull him closer so I could grind into him. Feeling how hard he was, I bumped and rubbed my groin over one of his thighs until I thought I could almost come...

'Chrissy, sorry, my darling, time for the second set.' He stepped back, adjusting his jacket and running his fingers through his dark curly hair, then reached for my hand. I let him lead me back into the bar. I was on automatic pilot. Second set? We'd hardly made it past first base!

Musicians. They're a different breed. Here's a blues joke. What happens if you play a blues record backwards? Your wife comes back, your boss tells you that giving you the sack was a mistake and your dog doesn't die. Laugh? I nearly started. Shall I tell you what's really funny about a blues joke? That blues musicians tell them to each other – and laugh. The second set meant that they were on stage again, after their drinks break and this time, instead of just instrumental music, there was a singer, a black girl called Maryze. I tried not to look daggers at her, in her sparkly red dress, but it was difficult. She was onstage with my man and I wasn't happy about it. She could sing though, I had to give her that much.

When the second set was over, Paul came straight to me. 'Chrissy, I have to help the band break down. Give me your number, I'll call you. No, even better, meet me tomorrow. We've got a lunch-time gig at the Third Tun in Greenwich – I'll take you to dinner afterwards.' He smiled his melting smile and I smiled back, but inside I was crying. I was going home alone. He was going to help the band break down, and I was going to go home and break down all on my own.

That night I sat on the sofa, drinking Southern Comfort and listening to Janis Joplin. 'Oh Lord, Won't You Buy Me a Mercedes Benz?' she sang. There's a line in the song about the Lord buying her a night on the town – I smiled bitterly when I heard it. I'd had my night and I wasn't happy at all at how it had ended.

In my mind I kept seeing Paul with his sleeves rolled up, lifting speakers and carrying them out of the bar, while Maryze coiled snaky grey leads and packed them into a box. Whenever she bent down, the split in her dress showed everything from the South Pole to the equator – and she had worryingly good legs.

Janis got it right, I decided – she'd got no help from her friends and neither had I. A week ago I'd been a happy, if somewhat lonely, party girl; today, thanks to Jason, I was a downright miserable woman, shot through with jealousy and without a second head on my pillow for the night. I pulled the glass dildo from its cushion of cotton wool in the drawer but even that couldn't tempt me. I had the blues, did I ever have the blues.

The next morning though, the sun came up, I still had a job (as far as I knew), and I didn't have a wife to leave me or a dog to die, so I got on with life. I depilated my legs so I could give Maryze a run for her money in the smooth stakes and, while I was wandering around bow-legged in an old T-shirt, waiting for the cream to take effect, I sorted through the CDs I'd borrowed from Jason. I came up with Aretha Franklin's *Respect*. It was feel-good music, so I cranked up the CD player to maximum volume, put a hot oil conditioner on my hair and pulled open the wardrobe door. I needed RESPECT all right, and I was going to get it!

An hour later I was in a taxi on the way to the Third Tun. I'd pulled the fur collar off the black coat and tacked it onto an old Chanel knock-off suit in houndstooth check – the way it was cobbled together wouldn't last long, but it wouldn't have to. The skirt was short and tight and, remembering what Jason had said about being cool, I'd set aside the suspender belt. Instead I'd opted for sheer black tights and, over them, shiny black boots. The shirt I wore was brilliantly white and crisp – I'd sprayed it with so much starch it could have cut butter. I'd found a deep-red lipstick and some pale matte foundation; together they gave me the vampy face of a 1920s film star. I looked sharp, I looked cool, and I was ready to sing the blues.

When I walked in the pub, every head in the room turned. I watched men looking me up and down, and up again, and I felt a warm glow in my soul and an even warmer heat between my legs. So much admiration was more than an aphrodisiac, it was like sexual rocket fuel. I could feel I was giving off vibes that had guys adjusting their clothing and pulling down their shirts and sweaters to hide their hard-ons. I might be cool, but to these men I was hot! I ordered a gin and tonic – no more cat-piss alcohol for me – and sat down at a table near the stage. When I crossed my legs, I heard half a dozen men gasp and splutter.

One of the Symposium appeared on stage, twiddled a few things and then disappeared. A few seconds later I saw Paul looking out from the stage curtains, but I pretended I hadn't noticed – cool and slow, cool and slow. One of the men who'd been standing at the bar shuffled over. 'Is anybody sitting here?' he asked, indicating the chair next to me. I looked him over slowly: on any other day he would have been a good catch, but today I wanted Paul to feel like I'd felt last night so, although I smiled into his eyes and said, 'Doesn't look like it to me,' I was watching Paul from the corner of my eye and saw how his mouth tightened as the guy sat down.

By the time Paul made his way out front, my companion had become bold enough to ask me if I was 'Uh, like, a big kind of, uh, blues fan,' and I'd told him I was really only a beginner but willing to learn; I could almost see the steam coming out of his ears. Paul appeared behind me, with his sax slung over his shoulder. 'Chrissy,' he said, bending down to kiss me on the side of my neck, 'how wonderful to see you, and how wonderful you look.'

I let him lead me to the back-stage area, waving goodbye to my former table mate as I went. But before we got to the changing room, Paul dragged me into a gloomy corner, already inhabited by a dusty fire extinguisher. He started to kiss me and I joined in enthusiastically. As I'd already gathered, he was an expert smoocher, no tonsil strangler, but one of those men who snogged slowly and thoroughly, as though kissing was the point of the exercise, not simply a stage on the journey. I let myself slide down against the fire extinguisher, it was getting difficult to stand up properly and I couldn't see the point in wasting my energy on it when I could devote myself to enjoying Paul's mobile lips and the way his fingertips were working their way inside my jacket, unbuttoning my shirt and easing their way under my bra straps, pushing down on the elastic fabric to free my breasts. His head descended and I felt the heat of his mouth travelling my neck and down until his teeth nipped gently on my right nipple. I was more than ready, and I was already hoisting up my skirt and reaching for Paul's flies when I remembered the tights. There was not a hope in hell of getting them off elegantly, not in a corridor anyway, and I didn't fancy hopping around in semi-public view, trying to extract myself from my hosiery, so I did something I hadn't done for years – I pushed Paul away. His eyes were dark with lust and my red lipstick was around his mouth as though he'd been eating cherries; it looked bloody sexy, to be honest. But I took a deep breath, shrugged my bra back into place and smiled up at him as I wiped the lipstick off his chin.

'Didn't you promise me dinner?' I said.

His smile was hungry. 'Of course, my place, after the show.' He brushed his fingers across my face and headed down to the changing room, from where I could hear other members of the Symposium bickering. I turned around on my spaghetti-weak legs and sneaked into the women's toilet to adjust my face and clothing. Once I was in a cubicle, I allowed myself to think about what had just happened: Paul's gentle insistence, his delicious kisses, the appreciative way his fingers lingered on my skin ... it was all a bit much and I pushed the horrible tights down around my ankles as I leant against the cubicle door and felt the cold air on my thighs. It wouldn't take long and, once done, I'd be able to face the punters in the pub more easily. The idea of sitting out there now, watching Paul on stage, while I was this hot and troubled, was too much to bear. I leant forwards, lowered the toilet seat, and put my bag on it to be safe from the kind of sneaky bastard who steals from your bag if you put it on the floor in a toilet cubicle. Then I slid both hands up my thighs, feeling my inner muscles jump and flex in anticipation of what was coming next – me!

There was one trick I was rather fond of, which I have to admit is not your usual, but each girl to her own, and right now I wanted some fast, furious and above all complete gratification. So I pulled up the tights again, unlocked the cubicle and scooted to the basin, where I ran cold water from the tap over my right hand until it was red from the chill. Then I went back into the cubicle, where I locked the door, leant against it, pulled down the tights with my left hand and – whammo! Three icy fingers, like Jack Frost: chilly, thrilling, fucking wonderful. It feels like somebody else's hand in you, that's the first thing, and the second thing is that it scorches – don't know why, but it does, burns like fire, even though it's cold. It's a gorgeous feeling, but you have to be swift so you get off before your fingers warm up. No problems there though, the problem was going to be hanging on long enough to get all the pleasure I wanted. I let my hand move a little, sliding in and flexing, preparing myself for what came next. I let my left hand drift over my bikini line, as if I really wasn't sure I was going to do this and then let my left index finger slip and slide down, until it hovered just over my clit. My right hand was throbbing as it began to warm up, which wasn't suprising, given how hot I was, and it was going to take only the tiniest touch, the merest little caress, for me to come.

Then I heard the main door to the lavatories open. I bit my lip. Somebody came in. I could feel my fingers getting warmer and I really wanted to come now – whoever was out there might spend ten minutes doing their hair or fiddling with their make-up; I should know, I'd done it often enough myself, and I wouldn't, couldn't wait that long. I pulled my bottom lip deep into my mouth, pressing my teeth into its inner cushion and let my left index finger circle my clit. I didn't groan, although I wanted to, but I did inhale pretty sharply. I pressed my head back against the cubicle door in an attempt to stifle my responses and the woman outside began to sing quietly. It was Maryze. It was pretty unmistakable, not only because she expressed herself in a beautiful deep bluesy voice, but she was singing a famous old Etta James song – probably the only blues song I could have named before this week – 'I Just Want to Make Love to You'.

I wasn't going to let Maryze deprive me of my rightful pleasure, so I waited until she hit the big line and let herself go with a rolling 'love to you ... love to you...' and I pushed deep with my right hand and circled with the fingers of my left hand and bit back even the slightest sound that might have given me away as I came. Then I stood silently until my legs stopped shaking and my breathing returned to normal before pulling up my panties and tights and unlocking the door. At some point Maryze had stopped singing and left the place, but I'd been too lost in the aftermath of my orgasm to notice exactly when it was. I washed my hands and repaired my face and headed back out into the bar.

I took my seat back at the table and watched Paul perform. Whatever relief I'd given myself, he'd been denied and, if I still felt horny, he must be positively insane with lust. At one point, when the Symposium moved into 'Blueberry Hill' and he came forwards to play a solo on his golden horn, I was glad I was sitting down. His eyes were fixed on me and when he knelt down, tipping his head back and lifting his saxophone high, it was exactly as though he was on his knees in front of me. I could almost feel his tongue inside me, so it was no suprise I was finding it hard to sit still.

I couldn't wait for the gig to be over. Even when Maryze appeared and started to sing, I barely noticed – all I could think about was that we would soon be on our way to Paul's flat.

It seemed like Paul couldn't wait either. There was no waiting around at the end of the second set, or helping the rest of the band to break down: he handed his saxophone to the bass player, stepped down into the audience, took hold of my elbow and led me straight out of the bar, even before the punters finished applauding.

He drove a canary-yellow MG. Well, what else? It was a sexy funny car for a sexy funny guy. On the way to his flat he told me musician jokes, except musicians call themselves musos, not musicians. I smiled, but really I was wondering how long it would take to get to his place and whether I should let my hand creep up his thigh, but he was driving so fast I was nervous about distracting him and, although he talked fluently, he never took his eyes from the road.

He lived in West Kensington – a little mews flat with a tiny garden, which I glimsped out of the window before he grabbed me by the shoulders. I stared up into his eyes while I shrugged out of the little Chanel jacket with its big fur ruff, and undid the cuffs on my shirt. Then I lowered my eyes to my front as I began to unbutton the crisp white front of my shirt. I heard him make a sound, like a little growl, and then he picked me up and half threw me onto his squashy sofa. It wasn't a cool move, or a slow one, but I was past caring – I pulled him down on top of me.

There were a couple of seconds of confusion while I tried to continue undoing my top and he tried to help me, and then he got the idea and started to pull off his clothes with one hand while tugging at my skirt with the other. I leant forwards to unzip my boots and he lifted my shirt off my shoulders. Then he pushed me backwards again with his lips nuzzling into my breasts. I reclined, trying to lift my leg in the air so I could remove my boot, while developing a sudden inclination to breathe deeply and a total inability to focus or concentrate: he really did have the most amazing mouth!

Finally though we got ourselves sorted out. I got both boots unzipped and my tights off, he struggled out of his jacket and shirt and then scooped me up again and carried me to the bedroom. I was a little peeved, to be honest. I quite fancied making whoopee on his cushions, but once I hit his big white bed, with him working his way with fingers and tongue down from my cleavage to between my legs, I forgot to be anything except achingly wet and completely pleasured.

Paul took everything slowly. He crept his way down, pausing every few seconds to revisit some tiny fraction of my flesh that had got a more than usually vocal response from me. I could feel myself melting underneath him – I'd never really known what 'melting' was before, but if the fire brigade turned up now and told us the building was on fire, they'd have had to carry me out in a tub, I was too liquid and boneless and without a will of my own to do anything.

The first orgasm happened before I'd even unzipped Paul's trousers. There was a moment when I remembered myself enough to get on with trying to give him back some of the fun he was handing out to me, and then his tongue hit exactly the right place and exerted just the right kind of pressure at the perfect speed and I was riding a wave of absolute physical glory. Even then, Paul didn't let it happen fast. He kept me there, right on the edge of coming, until I thought I was going to scream like a steam train whistle, and then he let me tip, slowly, over that edge. I did scream. At least I think I did. I can't remember too much about what I did; I was too busy being overwhelmed by what I felt.

The next orgasm I did remember more clearly. It came when I was on top of Paul, having slid him inside me as soon as he'd fitted a condom, which he did with expert speed; he was a man whose fingers were pure gold. I was kneeling over him, smiling down, and he was grinning up at me. 'Is this dinner?' I asked.

'This is simply the appetiser,' he said, and I started to giggle, and the action of laughing started something off inside me that he spotted immediately, and he began to thrust a little faster, while guiding my hand between my thighs. I leant forwards even further, so my breasts were rubbing against his chest, and let my fingers dabble against my clitoris, and then, just as I began to come, he pulled down and away from me, leaving me hovering on the brink of orgasm again. Over and over he brought me right to the screaming point and held me there, and then finally, when I thought I couldn't bear it any more, he tipped me over so we were lying on our sides facing each other. He pushed my hand away, replaced my fingers with his own and then made me come, gazing into my eyes as he did.

The third time I came, he was on top of me, kissing and biting my neck as I arched my back to push myself against him, and the fourth time we were beneath the covers of his bed, making a slow weaving rhythm of our bodies in the increasing darkness of the early evening. I drifted off to sleep to the sound of a blues tune being hummed in my ear.

When I woke I asked him what it had been.

' "Things 'Bout Coming My Way", by James Youngblood Hart,' he said.

I pretended to swat him, but I was too exhausted and happy to make the blow connect.

'I have actually got some dinner,' he said. 'Tapas stuff from the deli and *dulche de leche* ice cream for pudding. I thought you looked like the kind of woman who would enjoy ice cream.'

I nodded.

'I'll put the tapas on a tray, shall I? We can eat

in bed. Um, I wondered if you'd like to come to Dublin next weekend? We've got a gig over there.'

I nodded again.

While he was in the kitchen I thought back to the past few hours. The sex had been fantastic. It would be even more fantastic when I could persuade him to use the time between sets to invest in some quick and dirty knee-trembling behaviour, but there was no rush – we could take things cool and slow.

Carmel Lockyer's story, *Going Down on the Blues*, appears in the Wicked Words collection *Sex and Music*. She has also had another story published in *Sex and Shopping*.

Priceless Mathilde Madden

I love the idea of men for sale. Always have. Always will. And although its hard to pinpoint *exactly* why, I think in a nutshell, it's just, when I think about men selling themselves – in any context really, in any sexual context – something deep in my soul seems to sing. Just the thought of it. Men selling themselves. Selling their bodies. Selling their faces, their chests, their arses, their cocks. Offering themselves up to the highest bidder. Displaying their bodies for evaluation. Offering anyone who has the cash the chance to own them for a night. It's such delicious objectification. It's so very hot.

But an ordinary woman like me, with a very ordinary life, doesn't get the chance to experience such things very often. If ever. And even if I did run into some kind of sexy-men market stall on my way home from work, well, I kind of have this boyfriend anyway, so it isn't really on the cards.

So it's nothing but a hot idea really. I never even dreamt I'd put my money where my mouth is. But then my friend Kate starts talking about organising a Charity Slave Auction for the organisation she is working for. And, boyfriend or no boyfriend,

I can't help entertaining very unhealthy thoughts about what that might entail.

Talk about divided loyalties. Especially for someone like me. Someone, that is, with no willpower whatsoever. So, actually, divided loyalties, not so divided. Because, you know, I can just go and watch, I don't have to actually bid, or anything.

And so poor Kate – who is completely ignorant of my crazy dirty fetish for men-for-sale – is pretty bamboozled when suddenly I all but beg her to smuggle faithless-me into her auction.

She has many – eminently sensible – objections. Like the fact that it's just boring work. Like the fact I really should be able to find something better to do on my birthday. On my twenty-ninth birthday. Oh yes, because that's when the auction is scheduled to happen. Not exactly perfect timing. (Although, then again . . .)

'Look, babe,' Kate says when I've dodged about half a dozen very good reasons why not. 'Why don't you just go to the pub with everyone – Rex and Pete etcetera – and then go on to a club or something and I'll come and join you when I'm wrapped up. I'll be there by midnight.'

'It's not that, Kate,' I say, in the voice of a three-year-old child who isn't getting any more sweeties. 'It's not that I want to be with you, personally. Well, I do, obviously. But that's not the thing. The thing is I really, really want to come, really –'

'Don't be stupid,' Kate interrupts before I can actually explain. Not that I can actually explain.

Not to Kate. 'I can get you into much better events than this. What do you fancy? Fashion shows? Pop concerts? How about an awards show? I could do that, really I could. I know some people at one of the banks that sponsor the Brits and –'

But I manage to stop her there with nothing but a frown and I'm-so-not-that-kind-of-person eyebrows. 'Kate, please, I just want to go. Call it my birthday present. I –'

Kate interrupts again, 'But I don't get it. Why do you even want to come and bid? I mean, you have a boyfriend, Rex, remember? Why not leave the lovely auction lots for us single girls?'

I grin, sheepishly, but then try to give Kate a don't-be-daft expression. 'I'm not going to bid, Kate, I just want to watch. Bit of eye-candy fun. On my birthday.' And I do actually mean that. I do just plan to watch. Really.

'Well, OK, if you really want to,' she says with a sigh and a sort of shrug.

So I never actually do tell her why I want to go so much. I never have to let my kinks out of the bag.

OK, I know it's only for fun. No one is really paying for the men themselves; no one is really paying, well, for sex, but just the idea of it – the men showing themselves off, the women bidding.

Have I made it clear that I find this so fucking hot?

Then, I have to have this conversation. One evening, about a week before my birthday, I'm in bed with my boyfriend, Rex, and we've just had an excellent shag with loin liquefying kinky bits and everything, so he's in a pretty good mood, and I say, 'Rex, you know my birthday?'

My beautiful Rex is sitting up in bed looking somewhere between iconic and gorgeous. He's smoking a cigarette and he's still wearing the scuffed-up pair of black cuffs that I used to tie his wrists to the headboard earlier. His orangey-red hair is sticking out all over the place like some kooky kind of sculpture. He blows out an endless blueish-white plume of smoke before saying, kind of fast, 'It's next week and I've not forgotten.'

'I want to go to Kate's charity slave auction,' I say.

'Yeah,' says Rex, nodding sagely, 'I kind of reckoned that you might. How many are you planning on buying?'

I pick up my pillow and whap him with it. 'None! God, I do have some self-control you know.'

'Yeah, now you say that, but what's actually going to happen when you're there and there are all those gorgeous men parading about for you, up for grabs, and you've got your birthday money burning a hole in your handbag, are you even going to give a thought to poor old me? Stuck at home? After the years of sterling service I've given?' And he shakes his outstretched wrists in my face, so the manacles jingle.

Because, although there are some things that you might not really want to tell one of your closest friends – like that fact that you are super kinky for men selling themselves – it's different with your boyfriend. (Really it is. If you don't agree, you're wrong. I say, tell your boyfriend about your kinks. All of them. Asap. It is so worth it.)

So Rex knows. Actually, Rex likes. Actually, Rex even takes part in pay-for-play role play on occasion. And so, it's not really surprising that Rex saw this one coming.

'You don't trust me?' I say, enjoying the jingling cuffs and put-upon expression in spite of myself.

Rex laughs. He does find my dirty little secrets amusing sometimes. 'It's fine,' he says, still enjoying himself, 'we'll do something just the two of us afterwards.'

And I notice a naughty light in his eyes then. 'What are you thinking?' I say, intrigued but rather worried.

Rex smiles. 'Ooh no,' he says, 'can't ruin your birthday surprise.'

So, on the evening of my twenty-ninth birthday, I'm sitting here, surrounded by smoky clatter and chatter, in a very cramped room above a not particularly nice pub. I'm all on my own, and just starting to get an odd little tingling feeling in my stomach. It's partly excitement and partly a bit of oh-my-God-I-might-not-have-done-the-right-thing doubting. I could be with Rex right now, having a romantic dinner, or in the pub with a huge crowd of my closest friends and hangers-on. And although I have been having lurid fantasies about this evening for (what feels like) my entire life, I can't help worrying. What if it isn't any good? Oh, God, what if it doesn't turn me on?

After I've finished two nervous G and Ts Kate finally appears, looking elegantly harassed – as only Kate can.

I smile, woozily. I'm just a little bit zoned out because I've come straight from work with nothing proper to eat (and, of course, because I am stupidly over-excited about this event), but I tell Kate it's all going fabulously from my front-of-house perspective. And that's when Kate drops a small but perfectly formed bombshell. All her protests about my presence here – and particularly her concerns that I oughtn't to be bidding seem to have gone out the window. And birthday or no birthday, I can't just wallow on Fantasy Island – I have a job to do. Apparently.

Kate slides onto a stool opposite me, sets down her drink and then quietly confesses. 'Charity Slave Auctions aren't really in vogue any more,' she tells me, over the rim of her slightly greasy glass. 'You know, it kind of has sordid associations. But there are so many hot guys who work for Fur Fighters – I just couldn't resist. And it's not like they're actually prostituting themselves, is it? Not really. I got eight lovely meals donated, you're actually bidding on the meal out. See?'

'I see.'

'Anyway, the thing is, I kind of sold the idea to the board of trustees on the grounds that it would bring in shed loads of cash. So it bloody better.

Actually that's more or less what they said – only in rather more hoity-toity voices. So the money will talk. I hope. Well, it'd better do if I want them to keep employing me to organise events.'

'Well, it's pretty full,' I say, giving the room a quick once-over head sweep. And it is. In fact the room is heaving. Most of the occupants are women, but I can see the odd male face dotted around too and I wonder if they are here to bid themselves or have been reluctantly dragged along.

'Yeah, well, I know I was a bit obstructive – but actually, I'm really glad you're here,' Kate says, looking rather sheepish. 'I know it's your birthday and everything; I know I should be doing things for you, but, well, I was wondering if you could do me a little favour?'

Kate bends down and roots around in her handbag for a second, before straightening up to present me with a sizeable brown envelope. She slides it across the table.

I open my mouth to speak, but think better of it and instead take the envelope and peek carefully inside. It's full of cash. I open my mouth again, but Kate beats me to it.

'Two hundred and fifty quid,' she says. 'I don't actually want you to spend it, just, you know, keep the bidding going. And if you end up buying then, well, you're covered.'

I frown at her. Thinking of a hundred and one reasons why this is a bad idea. Not to mention an unethical one. Deliberately driving up the bidding

– isn't that the number-one auction crime? And what kind of birthday present is a stack of cash I'm not actually meant to spend? But really my main concern is: 'Kate. I can't bid in this auction. What if I win the bloke? I mean, Rex. You remember, my boyfriend.'

Kate looks annoyed and doesn't notice my mimicking of what she said to me a few weeks ago. 'I've explained all that though. You're just bidding on the meal. If you win the bloke you've got the money to pay, and then you can just go and have a nice meal. But really, if at all possible, try not to win the bloke. There's no profit in it if you win.'

So, well, talk about Kate changing her tune. And really, where does this leave me? Stuck in a room where an auction of apparently gorgeous men is about to take place, where I am duty bound to bid on any specimen that might not be generating enough cash – but if I win one of them I have to quietly go and have dinner with him and his gorgeousness (and the fact I own him) without any untoward behaviour. On my birthday!

But before I can say anything Kate stands up – apologising again, and muttering about not wanting anyone to see us talking – and walks out.

I sit dumbly at the tiny table, clutching my envelope like it contains Weapons of Mass Destruction. And then the room goes dark.

* * *

When she takes to the stage a few moments later, I have to say, Kate does her job really well. She prowls around the stage in her tight hot-pink dress, whipping up the crowd into what can only be described as a hormonal frenzy. Behind her, on a line of wooden chairs, the eight men she has on offer look really quite alarmed.

She introduces the charity, giving a sparky spiel about animals and fur – the former being good and the latter being bad. But before we tire of her contractually obliged waffle about the worthy cause, Kate switches gear. 'So now, ladies and ... can I see a few gentlemen here too?' She holds up a hand to shade her eyes from the spotlights and peers into the audience. From the back of the room several masculine cheers greet her.

Kate laughs in response and then gets back to her patter. 'Excellent. Now, I want to see some high bids this evening. We've got a meal for two for each winning bidder and their prize. So bid early, bid high and don't go home empty handed.' Kate plants her tongue firmly in her cheek as an excited cheer hits her.

The first specimen she has for us – and that is the way she puts it, specimen – is Jonathan, from finance. Jonathan is lovely looking, wearing a navy-blue suit/navy-blue shirt combo that makes his dark skin look like molten Green and Blacks. I try not to lick my lips.

I don't need to assist with the bidding on Jonathan. He fetches £160, without even blinking. And in a far corner of the room a table full of girls scream with excitement as their prize weaves his smiling way over to them.

And the ever professional Kate (anyone would think she auctioned off men every single night), rattles on to the next guy – Simon, from IT.

Simon, likewise, is gorgeous. He's a master class in blond spiky hair and a sun-breaking-from-behind-the-clouds grin. Kate wasn't joking when she said she had some hot men in her office. They're delicious. It seems like she's pulled a master stroke with this risqué auction – she's going to make bundles.

When Simon, along with a rather nice meal for two, is sold for another hundred quid or so, I settle back in my chair. I don't have to even think about the furtive envelope on my table, Kate doesn't need little old plan-B me.

But that's where I'm wrong.

The next chap, Keith, isn't quite as drool worthy as Simon and Jonathan. He's not bad looking, but he's not an oh-my-God, head-turning, is-that-guy-a-model-or-what type. And he goes for just thirty-eight quid, before I even have a chance to step in and unethically force up the bidding. Kate flashes me a glare.

So I'm sitting up straight and paying extra attention to the next guy, and when I see him, I forget to breathe for a second. He's kind of gawky. Rangy and red haired. He looks cute, but a little shy. He's actually blushing. And I think it's the blushing that does it, far more than Kate's evil glare – I bid.

And that's where the trouble starts, because my cheeky funny guy might not be America's Next Top Model, but there's something about him, and at least one other person in the audience has noticed it too, and that's all it takes. And then it's just like every eBay auction I've ever participated in – once I've put in a bid on something, I'm committed, it's mine. I've got to have it. And I have to have this guy. It's war! The bidding gets fierce between us. And Kate does nothing to cool things down.

I suppose I might have stayed in control, might have maintained my dignity and bowed out at two hundred quid, say, if it hadn't been for the fact that my guy was wearing very tight shorts that left nothing to the imagination and was quite definitely erect as soon as his price went past fifty pounds. Yum.

And I'm not sure quite what it is yet, but something about that tell-tale bulge tells me this guy could be very interesting. Even more interesting than his bashful stage performance would suggest.

And I guess that's why I'm still bidding even though my brown envelope limit has been long passed. That's why I'm bidding £380. That's why I'm getting out my cheque book and writing a cheque to make up the shortfall from Kate's cash.

And that's why I'm heading out of the door

with my purchase and jumping into a taxi on the rainy street.

We don't bother to go and eat – whatever Kate might have drilled into us about the fact I was bidding for the meal. Sod that. We go straight to my place.

In my little flat with low, low lights and soft, soft furniture my purchase looks even better then he did on the stage. And the idea that he seemed to actually be turned on by being auctioned off just won't let go of me. In a way that's even sexier than the fact he actually was auctioned off, than the fact I bought him. I just keep thinking about how hard he got and how hard he blushed.

I love . . .

I don't know if I can even explain it. I love it when men have dirty little secrets. I love it when they are turned on by something nasty, something wrong, something that twists against what society expects a man to be. I love it when men want things like that. When they burn and throb to be brought down, owned, used. And, although I know there are plenty of men that get off on that kind of stuff and are happy to shout it from the rooftops, I love it when the guy in question is all conflicted by his deviant desires. Just like the blushing guy in front of me right now.

It's so delicious. He's so different from Rex, who practically vaults the furniture to get to the ropes in the bedroom and, although I love Rex, I love this new spin on naughty little sub-boy too. It's just adorable. And, actually, I'll probably enjoy this so much more if I make an effort not to think about Rex too much.

I offer my purchase wine rather than coffee, because it's actually still quite early in the evening, and he accepts in a slightly shaky voice that makes me feel all twinkly with excitement. He's even more bashful now – he's biting his lip and not meeting my eye, and I haven't even begun to press the point. Well, not yet.

'You like that I bought you?' I ask darkly, looking at him over the rim of my glass.

'Yeah. Kind of.'

Oh, God, and his face is just priceless. Perfect. He hates that I know it turns him on, that I have that little chink where I can dig and twist.

'And you like that I own you? Right now?'

'Well . . .' But his words die in the air. I wait for him to speak again, but, nothing. Everything goes quiet.

Time seems to stand still for a bit and then I get up from my chair and walk over to him, getting right in his personal space, reaching into his lap, trailing my fingers over a desperate hot erection. 'I think the word you are looking for,' I say, softly, 'is "yes".'

He doesn't reply, so I squeeze the bulge in his tenting shorts harder. He makes a gratifying little mewling sound then. And I smile. And he gets even harder.

So I take a handful of his T-shirt, gripping it in the middle of his chest and twisting the fabric into a bunch, and then – acting like a caveman or something – I use this makeshift handle to drag him into my bedroom, and throw him down onto my bed.

I climb on top of him, straddling his tight skinny body easily. He sprawls beneath me, prone, his arms stretched above his head. He could just be being casual, just lying the way he fell, just lying the way that is comfortable right now, but he looks exactly like he's positioning himself to be tied down. Naturally, I choose to imagine that he is hinting at me about what he would like next. Letting me know what he wants, but can't bring himself to say. And I choose to take that hint.

From a bag tucked under my bedside table I produce a familiar pair of well-used leather wrist cuffs.

My recent purchase looks at them with widening eyes.

'Have you ever been tied up?' I ask, surprisingly breezily.

'Um, nope.'

'Have you ever thought about it?'

'Um.' His face twists into a strange expression. I almost feel like he is trying to hide from me. To climb inside himself. Out of the firing line. 'Um, yes, I suppose,' he says, eventually. So reluctantly.

I hold his gaze. I don't have to say anything to let him know that that vague admittance is nowhere near enough.

'I've always thought it would be hot, OK. But it's also twisted and weird. It's fucked up!' He almost looks angry as he says this, but his voice is catching a little with arousal. He did put himself on sale after all.

There's no debate though. In fact I start to tie him down while he's still talking. I move slowly, buckling his wrists snugly into the cuffs and then fixing them to the eye bolts that have been part of my bed frame since forever. 'You like it though,' I say. 'You like it even though you know it's "fucked up".'

'Yeah-uh,' he says, his affirmative becoming a soft moan as he pulls a little against his restraints. 'Oh, God. Yeah. I really fucking do.'

And then he's tied, but not over-restricted. He can still squirm, which feels right. I push his T-shirt up until it is bunched around his armpits, and play about with his elegant chest. I tug a little at the sandy hairs there, just enough to make him squirm and roll, and give himself away.

Not just a submissive, but a pain slut. A pretty, pretty little pain slut. All rose-flushed cheekbones and hard, hard cock. Eager and confused and just far too precious. Priceless.

And once I realise that, I need to make him more uncomfortable. Need to. And I need to do it now. I want to see him hurting, twisting in pain. From the bag, I pull out a pair of silver nipple clamps and dangle them in front of his face. He shakes his head.

'Oh, no.'

'Oh, yes.'

'No. I can't. I don't want this. It's too much.'

'I don't think it's too much. I think it's just right. Perfect. And the thing is,' I say, gently stroking his chest as I speak, 'I get to decide, because I own you. You are bought and paid for and I get to do whatever I want to you.'

'No,' he says. But there's that crack in his voice again, giving away that delicious arousal that I know means he likes the fact I own him, really. He likes the fact I get to decide just how uncomfortable he is. 'I don't think it's really meant to work like that,' he continues. But any further protests die away as his breathing gets heavier.

'Yes it does. For us it does.' And I dip my head and kiss his left nipple, before securing it quickly in nasty jagged teeth. He moans as the jaws close, but he doesn't protest.

And he's harder than ever.

He is tied down and clamped now. Rolling around on my bed. Not really coherent. Ecstatic. And I'm feeling pretty good myself.

I know where I need to go next. I don't have any option. I'm so wet and I'm rubbing myself gently against his leg. His helplessness, his pain, his liking his pain and helplessness, his conflicted emotions about liking his pain and helplessness, all these things are working together to enhance my spiralling arousal.

I move back. I can't remember when his clothes disappeared but he's naked now, and his hard cock is still as obvious and needy as ever. I lift myself up and move over it. Repositioning and moving him inside.

And, oh, oh, wow! Too good.

I move as he moves. We both slide and glide. It's easy and good. Familiar. He's very hard and the pressure is right where it needs to be, nudging me, pushing me on. We don't have far to go. Either of us. But at the same time, I'm not quite there yet.

I release his wrists so we can both roll over – locked together – and I can watch him moving above me, his long thin body, elegant, powerful, my property. I feel like I'm falling as his thrusts push me down into the bedclothes. And as I fall, I start to soar. Right there. Good pressure. It isn't always this easy, but the build-up – weeks of it – have brought me to just the right place.

He thrusts again and it almost pushes me over the edge. I'm so close to coming now. I just need . . .

I reach up and grab the sparkling metal chain that connects his two nipple clamps. I hold it for just a moment – a delicious anticipatory moment – and then I tug. Not so hard, but hard enough. He cries out.

Oh, God.

I tug again, timing it right this time so his cry coincides with his thrusting.

Oh, yes. Oh, nearly.

I do it again. And then, the next time I do it, and he cries out in pain, I come so hard I barely notice him any more.

When I open my eyes – barely seconds later – I'm holding the nipple clamps in my hand. They're not connected to him any more. And he's slumped on top of me, panting.

I hold the clamps up, not realising for a moment how I could have come to be holding them. And then it occurs to me that I must have pulled the chain so hard as I came that I pulled the clamps clean off. Oops. I bite my lip. 'Sorry,' I say.

And then he lifts his head to look at me. His face is flushed, damp with sweat. But the smirk on his face says it all. He pulls himself up into a half-sitting position, resting back on one elbow and rubs his bright-red nipples, wincing at me. But it's so big and exaggerated a wince, it's almost comical.

'Sorry,' I say again, but I'm finding it sort of funny now.

Rex grins at me. 'It's not funny,' he says, looking kind of like it is.

'Yeah, OK.' And I reach out and rub my boyfriend's poor tender chest myself. My poor wounded soldier. My hero. The things he does for me.

'So?' Rex says, reading my mind. 'Good birthday present?'

I laugh – almost relieved that he has come out of character. 'You should get an Oscar,' I reply, a little laugh lighting my voice.

'That good?'

I shake my head, because I can't believe he

doesn't realise that it was. Actually, he probably does. He's probably just fishing for adulation. Well he's fishing in the right place, because I feel very, very adulatory right now. 'It was wonderful. It was . . . Oh! The way you play acted Mr Conflicted for me. That was the best ever! I really, really loved that.'

Rex laughs. 'Yeah, well, I got sick of you going on about how hot that got you.'

'I never thought you could pull it off, though, or I would have pestered you to do it ages ago.'

'Well, now you know I can, I'm just going to play that part all the time for you. No more of your usual Mr Kinky Slut Boy, no more draping myself over the back of the sofa for you and begging you to "please, hurt me", because, of course, you don't like *that*, do you?'

I swallow. Because I'm so fickle and much as I love Rex's new conflicted shy boy, his trademark Mr Kinky Slut Boy is so hot too. Mmm, that bad boy schtick. So good too. 'Well,' I say, hopefully, 'maybe I could, I don't know, mix it up a bit, mix and match?'

Rex shrugs. 'Well, there might be limits. I might have to restrict you to just one persona per playtime, you greedy girl, otherwise it could get confusing.'

Oh! He is beautiful. 'God, no wonder I nearly bankrupted myself for you.'

'What?' Rex looks a bit confused. 'I gave Kate a whole stack of cash for you to buy me with. Didn't she give it to you?'

'Um, yeah, but I kind of went a bit over the limit.'

'How much did you pay?' Rex asks, shocked, and he kind of swallows when he says it. Shocked and aroused. He likes. He likes talking about the fact I paid for him.

'Three hundred and eighty.'

'Shit! Sophie! I told Kate to stop the auction at two hundred and fifty.'

I laugh. I have to. 'And you actually thought she would? You poor naive little whore-boy. Kate saw the glint of my cold hard cash. Why do you think she even agreed to your plans?'

And, God, even though things are pretty light and I am pretty spent, I still get a tiny tingle when I call him a whore. Because, well, just because. I sigh and run my hands over his body, gently, but still with a kind of possessiveness that even the breaking of the fourth wall hasn't quite dissolved.

Rex moans gently. He's clearly still as buzzy as me.

'Tell me how much you paid again?' he breathes.

'Three hundred and eighty pounds.'

'God, so you wanted me that much? I hope I was worth it.'

'Oh, baby, you were priceless.'

Note: Sophie, Rex and Kate all appear in Mathilde Madden's Black Lace novel *Mad About the Boy*. She is also the author of the Black Lace novels, *Equal Opportunities*, *Peep Show*, and the forthcoming Black Lace paranormal werewolf trilogy, beginning with *The Silver Collar*.

Confessions Primula Bond

We'd only just stubbed out our cigarettes when Sister Mary and Sister Benedicta appeared in the twilight and started wafting across the shaved grass towards us.

'How do they know about our smoking den?' I muttered as we scrabbled about under the leaves of the weeping willow, shoving mints into our mouths and pushing the half-empty bottles of vodka down the backs of our knickers. We'd have to stand to attention, keep our hands crossed behind to stop the evidence clattering to the ground. There was nowhere else to hide the booty. We were the only pupils in the upper sixth still wearing our uniform. We were all eighteen years old, leaving school for good in a few days' time. Everyone else was wearing mufti – but my gang still wore our blue skirts and white blouses with pride.

That was all my doing. I was known as Angela the Angelic, mainly because I always looked immaculate. I was head girl, a real goody-two-shoes, or so they all thought. And I loved our uniform. A psychologist would say I felt safe within its boundaries. There was no need for me to face my demons while I was regimented by the sensible wool and hygienic cotton we were ordered to wear.

Au contraire, mate. It's the uniform that frees me. It *was*, still *is*, my personal demon in a heavenly world.

At school I tinkered with the look, and never got into trouble. I wore my pleated skirts either too long or too short, I buttoned my navy-blue cardigan up the back, I rolled my socks down to my ankles. I was the golden girl. Everyone copied my style. The more golden I was on the outside, the blacker my soul became.

'It's getting dark. Maybe the bell's gone for lights out,' Sally Smith suggested, pulling a twig out of my hair.

'The crows are flapping their wings! We're in for a bollocking!' one of the others squealed. But Sally was slowly tucking a long blonde strand behind my ear. I caught a slutty gleam in her eye. This wasn't the girlish expression of a long-held crush. I put it down to the booze we'd lately smuggled in for our midnight feasts. Except that I'd caught her looking that way even when we weren't breaking the rules. In a way that made my stomach loosen. In the library, at breakfast in the refectory, early mornings in the chapel – and now, in the fading dusk.

The branches of our hiding place rustled aside, letting in the fresh scent of grass cuttings, and Sister Mary and Sister Benedicta were standing there.

'Angela. We would like a word.'

'Oh, don't tell her off.' Sally stepped in front of me. 'She hasn't done anything wrong. At least, she's not the only one.'

'We know that.' The two nuns looked right through Sally, gazing at me in that clear, unwavering way a wimple forces you to adopt. 'She never does anything wrong. Angela's the golden girl, remember?'

I cringed in embarrassment. Not even Sally had called me that out loud. The nuns stepped round her and each took one of my arms. 'We just want to talk to her.'

I just had time to toss my vodka bottle to Sally before Sister Mary and Sister Benedicta took me away, back across the green striped lawn, round the side of the main building, right into the secret quarters of the convent where none of us had ever been. The dusty parlour where they led me smelled of wet newspapers and old tea, and I remember the thick sigh of their skirts as they sat me down and the way, when they shook back their wide sleeves to fold their hands, an old lavender kind of smell pricked out from the black folds.

The other girls and I used to imagine the horror of being a nun. No fun, no boys. No kissing, no sex. What it would be like to cover ourselves up for the rest of our lives. No frilly underwear, no fashion, no choice. No glamour. The rumour was that the nuns shaved their heads when they entered the order, but we could swear we spotted wiry black curls (the Maltese nuns) or waxy yellow fluff (the French *soeur*) or grey wisps (Mother Superior) peeping occasionally out of the stiff white borders of the headdress.

'Have you ever felt the call?' Sister Benedicta asked me a while later as I dunked my digestive into a watery mug of cocoa. The bell would go soon. Sally, as usual, would be waiting.

I knew what Sister Benedicta meant, but all I could do was open my blue eyes, all innocent and questioning, and let the wet biscuit hover over my lips. 'Sister?'

'The call to take the veil. To become a nun, girl. We think you have it in you. You have this aura –'

The laughter started to slide about, danger-ously, inside me. If I moved a muscle, it would escape in an evil cackle. I so wanted my friends to hear this. My eyes watered with the effort of holding it at bay.

'It's nothing to get upset about, Angela. Quite the reverse. Being called is the highest honour any woman could receive.' Sister Mary's hand was pudgy and white on mine. I'd been sunbathing while I revised for my exams. My hand, still holding the biscuit, was slim and brown. The biscuit started to bend.

'We just wanted you to know that we can help. This is a very special time for you. So there's no need to suffer, to keep it to yourself any more. You're one of us.'

'So all I have to do is surrender?' I parted my lips, flicked my tongue out to catch the biscuit, and swallowed it whole.

The nuns gave identical little nods.

I looked through the arched windows into the cloister, where rose bushes drooped. There had been no rain for months. Over the gothic gables, on the far side of the clock tower, I could still hear the drone of the gardener's mower as he painted green stripes all over the grounds before darkness fell.

He was godlike, the new gardener. Only ever glimpsed from afar, on the brow of a hillock or disappearing behind a tree. But he was curious. We reckoned he'd been told to cover up so our souls would not be corrupted by the tight, crotch-faded jeans and rippling six-pack we'd drooled over with the last guy. So mostly all we saw of this one was a distant head of blond curls, which bounced as the tractor bumped over the ground. His blurred features starred in many a private moment in the dormitory, when duvets rustled with the sensuous touches of female hands on female parts, the night punctuated by ragged sighs.

As he was the only male on the premises, other than the sickly chaplain, we could live with the dark shirt and trousers he always wore, so long as we could ogle those big masculine hands steering the wheel of the tractor, torment ourselves with wondering how those hands would feel roving over a young girl's fancy, watch those muscular legs scaling ladders to snip at ivy like a prince climbing
a tower. That brawny neck bending over the rake

as he cleared the gravel, now bending to slick his tongue between our open, waiting lips, snake over our young, yearning breasts . . .

'Angela? Are you content with that?' Sister Benedicta was speaking. I tried not to fidget in my chair, but my seat felt damp. 'It may seem cruel,' she went on, 'but we find it's best not to tell your friends. And we know that sadly you're an orphan. So it's best to come to us fresh, as it were, and pure, with no one trying to dissuade you.'

'I can't even say goodbye to Sally?'

'Especially not Sally.' The nuns pursed their lips, raising the palms of their hands slightly before smacking them down again. 'Best that you leave your worldly fellows behind, and join us straight away.'

The bell for bed was tolling. When she'd done waiting for me at our favourite secret rendezvous, Sally would see this as my betrayal. The tractor had stopped droning. Perhaps she'd get her revenge by being the first to seduce the godlike gardener, be deflowered rapidly and roughly before she left forever, burning with the satisfaction of knowing that I was permanently out of the running.

'I need to pray about this, Sister,' I said, putting down my mug. 'Can I go to chapel before I go to my room?'

'Cell,' corrected Sister Mary. 'And really, you should be accompanied –'

'Yes, of course you can go to chapel,' interjected

Benedicta. 'Just don't turn on the lights, will you? We don't want the girls alerted.'

'Candlelight will be fine.'

I bowed my head to hide my grin. It was all I could do to stop myself running out of the door.

Thank God, she was still waiting for me, hiding in the choir gallery. When I told her what the nuns wanted, she started to laugh.

'You're far too dirty to become a nun, Angela. You'll never rest until you've had a man. So why?'

'It'll be weird, maybe even fun.' I pressed my fingers on Sally's lips. They gave, parted a little. Her breath was warm. Now she was sobbing. 'It's only for a while. Obviously I'll be pretending to have a vocation. But I like it here. And I've got nothing else planned for the rest of my life.'

'What about me?'

'I have to go now.' I started to push her out of the door. The gate to the nuns' garden was ajar. 'Look. They're waiting to admit me into their fold.'

'You can always change your mind.' Sally was begging me now. 'Meet me here, on the last day of term. You can come home with me.'

'I have to stay with the nuns for now, Sal. But I promise I won't finally decide until then.'

I never kept my promise to Sally, because in the end the decision was easily made.

'Meet Father Michael,' said Sister Benedicta a week later, sweeping up behind me.

I was standing at a window under the clock

tower, watching everyone on the gravel drive packing their trunks and books into their parents' cars. My possessions had already been brought from my dorm and locked away.

Bang on time I saw Sally running towards the chapel. She wasn't wearing uniform. She looked stunning in tight jeans I'd never seen before, a cropped white T-shirt showing her flat brown midriff sparkling with a navel ring.

'I have to see my friends.' I jerked round to face my gaoler.

The nun was standing very close to a handsome man with black eyes that seemed to slice right through my clothing.

'Father Michael is our new chaplain, Angela. He's going to instruct you.'

As the gates closed us in and the solitary summer began, I tucked my long blonde hair under a stubby white veil. I wouldn't have to cut it off until I made my first vows. I looked more like a nurse than a novice, but that was surely an advantage. They gave me a sacklike grey dress. I put darts down each side so it pulled tighter over my breasts and emphasised my waist, but only subtly, so the nuns wouldn't be able to work out how the combination of veil and sombre dress was such dynamite on their new sister. I obediently donned grey tights, but I let them bleach in the sun so they became see-through.

And my days revolved around my sessions with

Father Michael. It wasn't the swirly, girly vestments he wore to say Mass that turned me on, but the cassock he wore underneath. The undergarment, so to speak, which he was left with when all that flamboyance was put away. When he was in private. When he was instructing me. The first man to instruct me, I mean *really* instruct me, though he didn't know it.

He was supposed to take my confession through the grille in the chapel, but after pleading a sore throat the first time, he let me come round to his side of the grille, into the warm corner of his sacristy, and this became, forgive the pun, a habit.

I loved the long black coat, encasing his torso like a glove, draping over his stomach, over the suppressed swell in his groin, flowing to his feet – oh, I still get horny thinking about it, thinking about the storming male beast, his demon, you could say, that I discovered, unleashed, beneath it. I loved that it was so totally forbidden. That *he* was so totally forbidden.

Side by side on our chairs, his a kind of throne, mine a little wooden stool, those colourful vestments hanging nearby, he murmured of the holy life I was about to enter while I leaned forwards, allowing my folded hands to chafe against his sleeve. I listened intently, blinking very slowly, knowing how long my lashes would look splayed on my tanned cheek. I inhaled his clean soap smell and the whiff of something else, something sweet, like wine. There were tiny black buttons all the way down the front of his robe and a silver cross rested on his chest.

I especially loved it when, becoming more relaxed in our conversations as the weeks went by, he would lean back and cross one leg over the other, so that I could see the tensing of his stomach and the working of his muscles, the flexing of his knees, the swinging of his ankle.

I'd thought the all-female environment would quickly pall, but it didn't. I could have been out there, with my friends, with poor Sally, with boys, enjoying parties, orgies even. Sex. But I wasn't. With Father Michael as my goal, my days of contemplation and chores passed surprisingly easily. I certainly wasn't ready to leave. Not until I'd had him. The scenario suited me just fine.

As I charmed the other nuns, my head drifted with delicious fantasies about the seduction, when it came. How brutally, tempted beyond endurance, my buttoned-up lover would take me, there amongst the candles and incense.

At night I lay on the narrow pallet in my cell, blocking out the prayers and promises of the day as I trailed my fingers up the soft skin of my thighs, forcing myself to keep it slow, resenting yet relishing the rhythmic, frustrated twitching higher up, hungry to taste the real, raw cock I was waiting for, instead of my urgently exploring finger or sometimes a banana or cucumber saved from supper.

As the phallic shape of my chosen dildo

approached, untangling the burnished hairs between my legs, teasing apart the soft folds, pushing up into the desperate darkness, I sometimes created a far more wicked fantasy, taking it much further. I imagined doing it to one of my sisters, asleep so near to me in their cells, crawling over them with a blunt instrument in my hands, making them gasp beneath their makeshift lover, or pictured them, particularly the younger ones, crowding round the sacristy window, peering through the grille as the heart-throb Father Michael reared over me, abandoning every last shred of sanctity, and became a rampant, red-blooded man thrusting into my arched, abandoned self.

The summer, though still trapped in heatwave, was moving luxuriously on. Soon the new term would begin, the gates would open, and Mother Superior would require a commitment from me. She would never get it, because by now I was so horny I was climbing the walls that enclosed me. It was no longer enough to pleasure myself. I had one burning aim. My holy grail was to have Father Michael. Yes, to corrupt him, and to have him, and to run away with him. I'd been subtle enough. No one, not even the man himself, suspected the real filth of my desires.

I started to ask him to hear my 'confession' two, sometimes three, times a day, and I wove colourful tales of my life for him to hear and to absolve. And instead of forbidding this excess of confession, the nuns applauded it, assuming that I was cleansing my soul thoroughly before the big day when I made my profession. How I laughed at their delusion, even while I was gritting my teeth, prodding my fingers inside me during the steamy nights.

But I'd had enough of the talking, the sitting a shade too close, the soft laughter, even the playful arguments. Oh, it was intimate, all right. I'd handled that perfectly. But I wanted more, I wanted to wrench aside his infernal goodness, feel his hands on me, and I wanted it now.

So one day, towards the end of August, when the sky was white with heat and the only cool place was the chapel, I ran to his room and hammered on the door. I was burning both with the heat of the day and with the desire balling up inside me. My lust was beginning to show. I'd caught some of my sisters looking at me in a strange way, very like the way Sally used to look at me. They ran their fingers over my dress, brushing my curves, admiring the way I'd altered the plain habit. They started to sit closer to me when we were sewing, nudge me and smile when we were shelling peas. And Sister Cecilia, an attractive woman about ten years older than me, occasionally tipped my chin up with her finger, held my gaze for a long time, then asked me if I had a fever.

And that day I said yes, because it was the perfect excuse. While they were all in chapel I prepared myself. I turned my dress round, so that the zip was up the front and easily undone. I covered this with my grey cardigan, and would plead the shivers if anyone wondered why I wasn't wearing the regulation summer blouse. The tights came off before I entered his room, to give me that dishevelled, desperate look. And I wore no knickers.

'I'm so afraid, Father!' I cried as soon as he opened his door. I ran to my little stool, shaking so much that I failed to balance properly and fell against him. The hot surge of triumph and excitement as he sat on his own chair and put his arm round me was enough to make me cream myself there and then. 'I can never become a nun!'

'Angela! This isn't like you. For heaven's sake what's wrong?'

'God will never forgive me,' I moaned into his shoulder. I eased myself into the crook of his arm, pressing my breasts against him and squeezing out a couple more violent sobs. One nipple caught against a hard button, and I gasped with the sharp, delicious shock. But I kept talking. 'The sin is too terrible.'

Father Michael's arm stiffened. 'What sin is that?'

'That I'm so unworthy.' I shook my head as if struggling with devilish voices. Then I punched at his thigh, aghast at my own wickedness. The muscle under the black cloth was rock hard. My fingers fell open, and I kept them there on his leg, lightly at first, while I watched, under cover of some residual sighing, that place under his robe which I was determined to rouse.

'How can you say you're unworthy?'

I hadn't expected him to argue with me. I'd expected it would take a lot more tearful unburdening and skilful teasing before he said anything at all. He was only supposed to listen.

I glanced up. I'd caught him unawares, that was for sure. It didn't look as if he'd shaved this morning. His cheeks were dark with stubble. The top buttons of his robe were undone, and I could see the dark hair curling at his throat. I flicked my stupid white veil away from my cheek.

'Aren't you supposed to be saying Mass in a minute?'

His hands came up to my shoulders. 'The new guy is doing it.' He gave me a shake.

'New guy?'

'I've been meaning to tell you. Just stop this nonsense about sinning. You're so beautiful, Angela.'

The breath stopped in my throat when I caught the look in his black eyes. They were literally burning. I could see myself reflected there, in miniature, and my mouth was open. His fingers were digging into me, radiating warmth through my bones. He shifted his legs, pulled me closer between them so that I fell right off my wooden stool and was half kneeling, half swooning in his arms. He started to give me an awkward fatherly hug, but I kept weakening, slipping across his knees so that he ended up lifting me and now I was pressed hard against his chest, his chin banging against my cheekbone. I curled myself round him, skin crawling with lust on the outside, the sexy core of me melting with desire deep inside. Then he held me away from him again.

'Such a pure face, those bewitching eyes, and that golden hair – you're too angelic to be a sinner,' he said. I watched his mouth. It worked as if he had something else to say, but he stopped and bit his lower lip. His teeth were very white. 'Both inside, and out. I'm sure you have nothing to fear.'

I waited for him to let me go, now that he thought he'd examined my soul, but he didn't. I made as if to fall back onto my own chair, but had to steady myself by holding on to his legs again, and he didn't move. Didn't push me away, didn't pull me towards him. His hands were still on me, on my arms now, my hands were still on his legs.

'I'm not a virgin, Father,' I said, lowering my eyes in shame, sliding my hands further up his legs distractedly as if to push away my sins. The black cloth wrinkled, but he didn't stop me touching him. 'I've had sex. What does the Bible say? Carnal knowledge. I know what it's like to have a man inside me.'

I was hot now, breathing hard. I could tell he was hot, we were drowning in a heatwave, the sacristy was stuffy, the windows were closed, and there was a knot of desire bubbling up just above my pubic bone, threatening to boil over.

'Go on.'

His voice rasped like raw silk on my neck as I

bowed my head. My hands had reached the top of his legs now, and he shifted them very slightly apart.

'And the worst of it is, I loved it, Father. I wanted more. That makes me very bad, doesn't it?' I looked up at his throat, and saw him swallowing hard, several times. I bent forwards, pressed my face against his, let my lips move against his cheek so that I could feel the harsh rub of his bristles. 'Or maybe that makes me very good?'

A great shiver went through him. 'I shouldn't listen to this. I've made arrangements to leave, Angela, before this destroys us. Let my successor hear this confession. I can't be near you any more.'

'You have to listen.' I ran my hands up his chest and hooked my fingers into his collar so that he couldn't get away. So that I couldn't have a rush of guilt at what I was doing. 'There's no one else I can tell.'

His hands fell from my arms and I panicked. I stayed where I was, leaning more heavily against him, but kept still. We could hear the anticipation ticking like a clock between us. His breath was in my ears. My lips, still against his skin, started to caress. Another violent shiver convulsed him from his groin right up his body. His hands landed on my hips. Didn't land. Fell, grappled, circled my waist, fanned out to clutch at my buttocks, as if he was fighting for purchase on a cliff.

I reached for the top button, took it between my fingertips as delicately as I could. The tiny disc slipped, wet from my sweat as my fingers trembled. My uneven breath was the only movement I couldn't keep under control.

'I need to tell you this, Michael,' I persisted, extenuating the torture. I undid the top button and he kind of choked. 'If I tell you how it happened, just that once, then maybe I'll stop craving it. I'll be pure. And you and I can start again.'

'Who was it?'

I clamped my lips just to the side of his mouth to quell my yelp of delight. Thank God, he wasn't trotting out the standard, rehearsed penances. I'd hooked his interest, no sweat. But now I had to think up my story, fast.

'It was a dare. Truth or dare, you know? The girls dared me, one night in the dorm.'

'They dared you.' His chest was heaving as if he had just run a marathon, but all power seemed to have left him. How long ago those silly nights in the dorm seemed now. Despite myself, despite the efforts of the nuns all summer to unsex me, I'd become a woman.

'I was only supposed to kiss him.'

I paused, squinting at the next button, slipping it out of its socket. He didn't move. His hands were rigid on the cheeks of my butt. I lifted my face as if begging to end my story, but there was his mouth. The word 'kiss' hissed in the air.

'A kiss would have been harmless, I suppose,' he muttered. He was looking at my mouth as if fascinated. I ran my tongue over it. I was thirsty, and so was he. In the chapel on the other side of the panelled wall someone struck a note on the organ. We both jumped, but towards each other. Our mouths met, the undulating surface of our lips electrified, drawn magnetically until we were licking, then nibbling, now biting. How can the speaking part of your face send such silent, fiery currents shooting through the rest of your body, sparking in your nipples so that they harden into nuts, searing down your belly until your fanny starts clenching with ferocious longing?

'But I knew it would be more than that when I crept up behind him, and we were all alone, and he was busy packing his tools away, how the girls laughed when I told them about the tools –'

'His tools? Who was it, Angela?'

I kicked the stool away. It fell with a clatter. We froze, wondering if anyone in the chapel had heard, but the organ was playing softly now, just the bass notes throbbing through the wall, and Michael yanked me roughly onto his lap, spreading my legs to grip around his.

'It was so exciting. I said something stupid about needing a can to water my window box and he wheeled round, saw me in my best nightdress, actually it's a petticoat, all silk and lace, I have it hidden in my trunk in the storeroom –'

'What happened? What did he do to you?'

Michael's hands pulled feverishly at my dress, pulling it up my thighs. As my hips and the golden hairs of my pussy were uncovered, the rough fabric of his cassock scraped me with a tender, half-painful friction. His hands were warm, kneading my bottom, still bumping me fiercely against him. And soon he would feel the dampness, dribbling out of me, right through the dark fabric still covering him.

'I kissed him, like this, like they'd dared me.' I held Michael's face and kissed him again. Already the taste of his mouth was familiar, and this time there was no hesitation. We wanted to eat each other. His long, strong tongue probed forcefully, and it was my turn to groan because there was a second phantom tongue, a phantom phallus, probing inside me, pushing me open, barging inside. My groaning echoed off the vaulted ceiling of the sacristy.

'Did he force you?'

'Oh, Michael. He was so sexy. How could something so good be so wrong?' I gyrated hard against him, and crooned out loud to graze the ridge of stiffness there, my prize. I started to rub myself back and forth along it.

'So he just took you? Threw you down, lifted your negligee, saw you naked –'

I undid some more of his buttons, delight bubbling up to see his broad chest and his stomach with its line of dark hairs marching south. I smiled, then I started to unzip my grey dress. Time to let the woman out. Time to show him the breasts nestling there, already swollen with desire.

'Threw me onto some sacks, yes, a pile of grass

cuttings. He didn't waste time, you know, being a gardener. No sweet talk, those types. But then I was ready for him. So, so ready.'

I cradled my breasts so that they nudged out through the zip, stretched my spine so that the dark-red nipples poked out and were inches from his hungry, wet mouth. 'He just undid his trousers, and showed me what he had, his penis, his long, hard cock, Michael. Like this. I just opened myself up. Like this. I wanted him to fuck me. Oh, it didn't take long, Father –'

'Don't call me that.' He tried to grab at my hands, but I twisted away from him, still fondling myself. 'Did you say "being a gardener", Angela?'

I raised myself up on my knees, bent over him, juicy fruit dangling right over his face while I undid the other buttons. He reached up tentatively, grabbed what was on offer, squeezed my breasts together, nipped and bit at the raspberry nipples. It was pure electricity. I ripped at the remaining buttons, arrived at the black boxers barely covering his erection. I allowed myself a lingering look, so near, so near now. I snatched down the shorts and it flung itself upright, quivering as if a wind was buffeting it. My body shivered to see it. But a crazed part of me still wanted to tease, torment, us both. I wriggled backwards so that I could bend down, ready to lick the beading tip.

'We didn't speak. I don't know his name.'

I sucked hard, drawing the rounded head past my teeth, and Michael fell back in his chair, totally powerless. In the chapel they were singing now. It was hot and heavy in my hand, Father Michael's member, it was bulging in my mouth. I didn't know if or when he'd done this before, but I wanted to please him. It sure as hell pleased me. As I sucked, his fingers wandered over every dip and curve, explored every crack and crevice he could reach. The pressure was becoming explosive.

'It was Raphael,' he said, tugging my head up. 'Oh, God. He's not a gardener. He just looks after the place until they find a replacement.'

I straddled him, hushed his mouth with my finger, keeping his length firmly in the other hand. The fairy tale was over as far as I was concerned. It was time for reality.

'I don't care what he is. I want to forget about him.' I brushed the bulging tip against my ready wetness. 'I've confessed all now.'

Michael's black eyes closed. For a terrible moment I thought he was going to push me off him, but not even *he* was superhuman enough to resist me now we'd come so far. I had him trapped. I rocked very slightly in a little dance, knowing instinctively what to do. He was sprawled helplessly beneath me in his throne. I played about a little more, preparing, tipping myself to guide my sex toy up, up, sliding it between the sensitive surfaces. That thick shaft was already wet from where I'd licked it. Now I wanted to slick it with my honey.

Not so helpless after all. Suddenly, he grabbed my hips and plunged me downwards. I actually groaned like an animal as the length of him rocketed up inside me, stolen inches of pure pulsating pleasure. I paused, nipples nudging his face as if they belonged there. He opened his eyes. He was a real man at last, a man who wanted to watch while he fucked me.

I started the stroke, up, down, no choice but to move, engulf him, every filling inch of him grazing every screaming inch of me so that I could only go so far before slamming back down, and each time we met I was wetter and he was harder.

We collided, over and over, in our sweet rhythm. Fire streaked through me, my breasts bounced frantically, his black eyes watched, and then it started, like all those other times with the cucumbers but ten times more powerful, it was rolling over me, I was arching to hold the sensation, trying as well to curb the inevitable, but it was shattering on its peak and flooding through me. His eyes were still on me as my body bucked and writhed. I was astride my mentor as he smiled slowly then pumped everything he had into me, throwing me upwards with the force of it.

I let out a long, low scream, disguised I hoped by the singing next door, and we rocked like we were born to this, thrusting and panting like we were fighting, his robe open to reveal that sacred, magnificent body, buttons scattered like sins, my virginal dress unzipped, and then, as the singing reached a crescendo, we raced towards our own crescendo until the keys banged down for the final chord and we shuddered and exploded together.

Oh, yes! Our coupling was every bit as unholy as I'd dreamed.

'Now we can be together all the time,' I murmured against his chest, soaked in his sweat. 'I'll stay in the convent, I'll take my vows, and we can do this whenever we like.'

Father Michael smoothed back a strand of hair that had escaped from the veil I still wore, zipped my dress briskly, and stood up.

'I told you. I'm leaving. Today, while there's a chance to salvage my career,' he said. He started to do up what buttons were left on his cassock. 'This can never happen again.'

'You don't mean that. I need you.' I grabbed at him. I wanted him to look into my blue eyes again. But he'd turned back into a priest. I throbbed and ached from where a man had fucked me, but that man was gone. I got down on my knees. 'I need you to – to carry on instructing me. What am I going to do?'

There was a knock at the door. Father Michael wiped his face with a pure white cloth hanging on a rail and stretched his arm to open it.

'It's not me you need to hear your confessions, if you're determined to stay in the convent. Any priest will do.'

There was a rush of warm air as the door opened, the scent of wood polish and candle wax drifting from the chapel.

I kept my position on the floor. Out of the corner of my eye I could see another figure in a long black cassock, framed by the doorway. His hair was blond and curly.

'And I think you know the new guy already, Angela.' My departing chaplain allowed himself one last, dirty laugh. 'Meet Father Raphael.'

Primula Bond is the author of the Black Lace novels *Country Pleasures* and *Club Crème*. Her next novel, *Behind the Curtain*, is published by Nexus. Her short stories have appeared in numerous Wicked Words collections.

Geek God Violet Parker

One of the good things about where I work, in fact the only good thing about where I work, is the fact we still have a proper tea break. At 4 p.m., everyone who fancies it wanders over to the staff-room and has a cup of tea (and maybe even cake, if it's someone's birthday). Some days, someone brings some entertainment, usually a stupid email to read out, or a saucy quiz, or something like that.

Today we have the best of both worlds: an email quiz.

'It's called the geek test, OK.' That's Mary talking. Mary is one of those people who like to be centre of attention. That's Mary's thing. I expect that's why Mary is always bringing stuff like this along to tea break. 'It's kind of like the purity test, you know that thing that tells you how much of a slag you are, but this one sees if you are a geek or not.'

In the corner, Chris, the fat IT guy laughs – half to himself – and then says, 'I bet I do pretty well.'

And then everyone laughs, because Chris is funny like that, and always sending up his blatant geekitude. That's Chris's thing.

Anyway, Mary starts reading out the questions

on the geek test, and we all laugh and raise our hands if we are guilty of the various crimes of geekhood. No one actually keeps score, but it's clear that Chris is raising his hand on everything, from 'Have you ever been to a *Star Trek* convention?' to 'Can you program in machine code?'

The test is quite long and, by the time Mary's on to the last page, there aren't that many of us left in the staffroom; just me and Chris and Mary, and also Caroline – my opposite in the Press Office – who has been smirking knowingly to herself for the entire test.

The last page is all about role-playing games. 'You know, like Dungeons and Dragons,' Mary says, which makes Chris snort in loud derision.

It soon becomes clear that Chris is, again, going to be the victor here. I sit behind my teacup with an amused grin on my face as Chris cheerily admits to 'Have you ever painted miniatures?' and 'Have you ever spent more than six hours in a gaming shop?' And we all laugh at that last confession.

Then Mary says, 'OK, nearly on to the last few here. Have you ever Larped?' Mary frowns. 'Larped?'

'Live Action Role Play,' Chris offers. 'It's like, ahem, Dungeons and Dragons, but you run about outside and act it out for real.'

'Gosh,' says Mary, 'well that's a new one on me.'

Chris raises his hand and smirks. 'Guilty.'

And that's when we all notice that Caroline has

her hand up in the air too. And that's when we all suddenly stop being interested in the geek test and start being interested in Caroline's murky past, because Caroline is one of those people who you can depend on for a really good murky-past story. That's Caroline's thing.

But Caroline is having none of our clamouring questioning about how a nice girl like her ended up doing a geeky thing like Live Action Role Play, because 'It's a long story,' and 'Tea break was over a quarter of an hour ago.' But we've got to know, and so Caroline suggests we meet in the pub over the road at 5.30.

Chris gets the first round in, making us swear that we won't bully Caroline into starting the story before he gets back. So we manage to contain ourselves, but the very second the drinks clink down on our sticky table, we make her begin.

She grins a saucy grin for a moment before she opens her mouth.

'Charlie Baker was fucking gorgeous. He had the body of an athlete, the face of a model and, as I was to discover, the brain of a geek,' she says, clearly relishing the looks of absolute concentration on our faces.

Caroline takes a sip of her drink and goes on. 'OK, so this was ten years ago, when I was at university in Sheffield. Charlie turned up in my psychology lectures in the second year. I knew he wasn't a psychology student so I asked around, and it turned out he was a computer science student and was sitting in on the lectures because he was into some kind of artificial intelligence stuff, or something dull like that. And that single boring fact seemed to be all anyone knew about him. Well, that and the fact that he had a smile that could melt knickers at twenty paces – not that he appeared to use it much.

'He always sat near the door for lectures and dashed straight off when they were done. I tried time and time again to sit next to him and get him in conversation, but he was having none of it. Always had to get back to the computer lab. Always so busy.

'He was like an iceberg. Not the nine-tenths under water thing, just, you know, the made of ice thing. And I'd basically all but resigned myself to admiring him from afar, when I suddenly got a lucky break.

'I was in the dark basement corridor of the student's union – a poky little rabbit warren, where all the clubs and societies have their little rooms – and I saw Charlie. He was right there – walking along the corridor in front of me. So I followed him, of course, straight down the rabbit hole. Or at least down the corridor, and I saw him disappear into a room, the door of which proclaimed it was the home of the "Gaming Soc".

'Now, I didn't quite have the guts to just follow him straight into the room. But luckily the student launderette was just across the hall. So I nipped in there instead, and staked it out.

'Well, I was waiting there, among the whirring

and the sudsy smells, for bloody ages. It started to get late. I started to get hungry. It began to look as if Charlie had escaped once again. But then the door of the Gaming Soc room opened.

'But it wasn't Charlie who came out of the room. It was Tom.

'Now, I knew Tom – the year before he had been in the same corridor as me in halls. He was an über-geek, little and nerdy with big thick spectacles and a strange twitchy manner. Basically, he was creepy, and I'd normally avoid the likes of him, perhaps even denying all knowledge of our previous connection. But at that moment I loved that connection with all my heart, because a connection to Tom – it seemed – was a connection to Charlie.

'So, I feigned coming out of the launderette, acted all long-time-no-see and the next thing you know I was walking down one of the many hills of Sheffield with him, towards the area where he lived, and I was pretending I was heading there too. And, with very little prompting, Tom explained all about the various delights of the Gaming Soc. They were into role-playing games, i.e. Dungeons and Dragons sort of things, and these games could go on for hours and hours. That's why Charlie had been in that room so long. Because Charlie, as Tom explained, was a huge fan of all things role play.'

Caroline picks up her smeary glass. 'Course,' she says, 'this put me off him a bit. He might have been God's gift, but he was also a total geek.'

She sits back at this point and takes a little sip

of her vodka tonic, but clearly not wanting to pause for too long in case she loses the floor.

'Hey,' says Chris, grabbing his chance, 'this is such a sweet story: what will win out? Caroline's prejudice or Caroline's lust? It's like Shakespeare.'

Caroline sighs. 'OK, well, truth is, it didn't put me off him that much, not really. I was just, well, just saying . . . he *was* a geek, but he was also just far too sexy a geek to be ignored. I wanted Charlie. And the only way to get to Charlie was clearly through this role-play stuff. He didn't seem to be interested in anything else. But how to find out about role play? There was no internet back then in 1994. OK, there probably was, but I didn't know how to use it.

'I only had one source of information: Tom.

'Two days later I was grabbing lunch in the dingy union bar and there he was, my source of information, perched over a burger and chips. I wove my way through the studyers and the skivers and plonked my tray down on his table, sliding on to a stool and grabbing hold of the conversation straight away by demanding to know more about the world of role play.

'I have to say that most of what he told me went in one ear and out the other – loads of stuff about orcs and dice and goblins. But then he started talking about this thing called live combat, or Live Action Role Play, and my ears pricked up then, because I saw the possibilities straight away.

'"So you go away for four days?" I said, trying

to sound as calm as possible. "Like on a mini holiday?"

'"Yeah. In fact we're going to Wales over the Easter vacation. I can't wait." Tom paused to pop a chip into his mouth.

'The very idea of Wales in April filled me with a soggy dread, but, well, Charlie! So I pushed on. "So, er, do you let beginners come along on these things?"

'Tom frowned at me as if he didn't exactly understand the question. Then he screwed up his face so he looked even more weasel-like than ever and said, "What? Do you want to come?"

'I nodded.

'And then he kind of blushed, but he looked really happy. "Wow," he said, "that's excellent. We always need more girls. You would make an excellent she-orc."

'My heart sank a bit at this; somehow, I didn't think seducing Charlie would be made any easier if I were dressed as a she-orc. "Do I have to be a she-orc? Couldn't I be an elvin maiden or something?"

'"Well, not really: this is kind of a battle – orcs versus barbarians. So you'd have to be an orc or a barbarian and there aren't really any female barbarians, so –"

'"I see," I interrupted, and then added casually, "is Charlie being an orc?" I said this while fiddling with my fork so it looked as if I didn't really care one way or the other.

'"Nah, Charlie'll be a barbarian. Charlie's always a barbarian. Got the build, see." Then Tom grinned knowingly at me. "I'm an orc though," he said with a certain relish. And then, I can't be sure – not sure-sure – but I think he winked at me.

'So that was that, it was all set. I told my housemates I wasn't coming on the planned holiday to the Lakes over Easter, because I had made plans for a little holiday of my own. And when I told them about it they tried, only half jokingly, to get me to go to casualty and get my brain checked out.

'And they might well have had a point because three weeks later I was in the back of a mini-bus rubbing damp thighs with the University of Sheffield's most spoddy ultra-geeks, and I wasn't even sitting next to Charlie.

'Not only that, I didn't even get to spend the four-hour-long journey to Wales staring at Charlie, who was looking particularly dreamy in tight jeans and a sort of furry gillet thingy over his cheesecloth shirt. I didn't get to gaze lovingly at Charlie because Tom decided I needed pointers and started giving me an impromptu tutorial on how to wield a sword in an orcish sort of a way.

'Something that included grunting, grunting in front of Charlie, which – however much he might be ignoring me – was so not fun.

'Somehow, though, I managed to grunt and snuffle my way through miles of drizzley motorway and into the heart of such breathtaking, crackly-fern-covered Welsh scenery. Brownish-grey hills rose up to meet greyish-brown sky in a way that was both beautiful and slightly depressing. I leant against the mini-bus to drink it in, inevitably picturing Charlie striding windswept across it like a lone stag. But I didn't get to enjoy this image for long, because I was quickly dragged off by Tom to help pitch the bloody orc tents.

'Standing in the rain, smashing tent pegs into boggy soil with a mallet, I was suddenly faced with the waterlogged reality of life under canvas in Wales at this time of year. I found myself fantasising about all the drinking and partying and cosy log fires in the Lake District cottage that I had sacrificed for this weirdness. In all honesty it was probably raining there too, but at least they had some bricks and mortar between them and the elements.

'Bloody Charlie, he'd better be worth it. And my plan (oh yes, I had a plan) had better work.

'Although gorgeous barbarian Charlie was on the other side – he was the enemy, as it were – that could actually prove to be to my advantage. My oh-so-clever-idea was that once battle began and the fake swords started to clash, I would engineer getting myself taken prisoner by Charlie, who would then, no doubt, take me back to his tent and ravage me in a barbarian manner, as the game demanded. See, I'd figured out that the best way to get some Charlie-shaped action was to make the action itself part of his passion, make it part of a role play.

'By the time I was standing, shivering, in a line of orcs, clutching my padded fibreglass sword, I could think of nothing but the fantastic Charlie-ravaging that awaited me (despite the fact that I had been rather unsubtly made up as an orc, with disgusting green grease paint). I could see my beautiful quarry in the opposing line, across the scratchy grass. It had finally stopped raining, but the sky was still a heavy grey, and he shone against it like a blond beacon. He was so beautiful, dominating the majestic landscape with a majesty all of his own, with his tousled blond hair whipping about in the squally wind. The furry thing and cheesecloth shirt he had been wearing earlier remained, but the tight jeans had been replaced by even tighter brown leather trousers – it was almost as if he were deliberately trying to get me excited.

'With a sudden urgency, a whistle blew and then all hell broke loose as the two opposing sides hurtled towards each other, roaring. I crouched low in the long scratchy grass and darted around in the crowd.

'Avoiding the swords and pikes and clubs actually turned out to be quite exhilarating. I rolled and dived around, my tactic of keeping close to the ground working very well. And as soon as I got within striking distance of my quarry, my delicious barbarian prince, I feigned a tumble and rolled around in the mud yelping.

'But Charlie didn't even seem to notice.

'And then someone – someone else – grabbed

me by the arm and bundled me up and over his shoulder.

'After some very uncomfortable travelling upside down across the grassland, I was dumped in a heap on the ground, behind enemy lines in the barbarian's encampment. Slightly stunned, I looked up into the face of my captor. He was a cute little thing. I was seriously surprised he had managed to run cross-country with the not insubstantial moi over his shoulder. He had rather floppy brown hair drifting into his eyes and, of course, he was wearing the standard barbarian uniform of leather and fur and bare biteable skin.

'"Hi," I said.

'"Don't talk," he hissed back, "you're meant to be a prisoner. I never got a prisoner before."

'"OK." And I know it sounds strange but just for a few tiny moments I must have forgotten all about wanting to be captured by Charlie, because I said, "Are you going to ravage me?"

'He laughed. "Doubt it. I probably have to give you to my commander."

'"Who's your commander?"

'"Charlie Baker."

'"Oh." Bingo!

'The downside of this great news was that I had to spend the next few hours in the prisoner-holding bay – which was actually just a large tent – until Charlie returned from the battlefield. I found myself a cosy spot near one of the paraffin heaters and settled in for the duration.

'In one corner, a large gang of the prisoners had

begun playing a separate game-within-a-game, setting up an elaborate and entirely different role play on the table, battling with tiny figurines.

'I sulked in my cosy corner, excited, yet bored.

'It began to rain again, storm clouds ushering in the evening before it was really due. I didn't know the exact time because watches were a big old anachronism and hence banned but, shortly after the heavens reopened, a worrying rumour started to go around the tent. It seemed several high-powered barbarians had been captured by the orcs and a Berlin Wall-style prisoner exchange was going to take place – which meant all ravaging was off!

'Obviously, my heart sank. The last thing I wanted was to be traded back to the ruddy orcs and end up having to get captured all over again. When I heard that one of the high-up types captured was Charlie himself, my heart sank even lower.

'Now I really couldn't win. I was trapped on the barbarian side, Charlie was trapped with the orcs! I kicked an anachronistic lemonade can on the muddy tent floor.

'But, despite my despairing mood, the prisoner exchange itself turned out to be quite exhilarating, despite the rain slithering down the back of my neck. We were all comically roped together and herded into a small woody clearing in the fast-fading light. Various negotiations took place in orc-grunts and barbarian-grunts, while I scanned the other set of prisoners until I saw a distinctive mass of blond hair and furry waistcoat.

So near, and yet so far. Dammit, I didn't even get to be on home turf while he was our prisoner.

'Making my way back into base camp, I found Tom was at my elbow, proffering a rather out of character orange cagoule. "Hi, Caroline, are you OK?"

'"Yeah, yeah," I said, grabbing his offering and pulling it over my orc clothes without breaking stride.

'"I'm sorry you got captured." He shrugged. "I meant to keep an eye out for you. Still, I got you back, didn't I?"

'By the time Tom was saying this we were already outside his tent. It was only then that I noticed that his tent was ever so slightly bigger than the others. I began to wonder about something. "Tom," I said slowly, "are you, like, in charge of the orcs?"

'"Um, not exactly," Tom said, looking slightly pleased I had asked. "I'm one of five commanders. But the prisoner exchange trick was all my idea."

'"Oh," I said, "thanks." And then I thought for a moment and said, "What do you mean by trick?"

'Tom smiled. "Oh yeah, you wouldn't know. Well, we didn't want to hand over Charlie did we? After all, he's one of their commanders. It's like, you know, having taken their queen in chess or something. So we pulled a little trick, got one of our tallest barbarian prisoners to dress up in Charlie's clothes, tied him up and gagged him and in all the scuffle it –'

'"Oh my God," I interrupted.

'"I know," said Tom, clearly swelling with the pride at the thought of his excellent plan. "It shouldn't have worked really, but it did!"

'I brushed his boasting aside. "Yeah, yeah, never mind that now. Are you trying to tell me that Charlie is still here?"

'"Yeah."

'"And he's our prisoner?"

'"Yeah."

'"And he's naked?"

'Tom looked at me, very puzzled. "Well no, of course not. He has his underwear on." He cocked his head to one side. "Caroline? Caroline, are you OK?"

'"I'm just fine, Tom," I said, in a very odd-sounding voice. "Very fine indeed."

'Night had properly fallen now. The boggy campsite that I was currently calling home looked different in the dark. It twinkled prettily in torch-light, like a squelchy fairy land.

'"Er, Tom," I said as we headed across camp to the big sort of main tent right in the middle – apparently there was going to be some kind of feast and celebration of today's minor victory. "Do you need anyone to guard Charlie?"

'"Guard Charlie? Nah, I got someone on it. Anyway, you've got to come to the feast – you're a part of it, after all."

'I cursed under my breath, but followed Tom into the tent.

'But after just half an hour – and that was all I could take of ale swigging and weird singing – I slipped out, determined to find out where Charlie was. Most of the camp was in darkness now, but I could see torchlight coming from the front of one of the tents. Hunching myself up against the drizzle (having lost my precious cagoule at some point during the feast), I headed in that direction.

'As I approached, I saw that there was a young-looking guy sitting outside it, sheltered by a small awning. Even by torchlight I could tell he had really terrible skin, which probably wasn't being helped by the caked layer of green orc make-up he was wearing. "Hi," I said breezily, "not going to the feast?"

'"Nah," bad-skin replied grumpily, "got this bloody job, didn't I?"

'"Oh, well, you know, I don't really go in for feasts all that much. I'd be happy to stand in for you for half an hour," I said, with all the breeziness I could conjure up under the circumstances.

'Bad-skin looked sceptical. "I dunno," he said. "If anything happens to him I'll be in dreadful trouble. He's a big prize. A commander, you know. Tom said not to leave my post for anything. Look." And by way of a horrible demonstration he produced from the shadows a plastic bottle that clearly contained urine.

'"Ew." I said, then shrugged. "Well, it's up to you, but if you let me take over, I promise I'll keep a very close eye on him."

'Bad-skin put down his bottle and fixed me with a glare, but I could tell he was wavering – how could he resist the ale and singing?

'"Well, OK then," he said eventually, "just for half an hour, but don't leave your post, whatever happens. And don't go in there either; apparently he has ways of talking to you to try to get you to let him go."

'And a few minutes later, once bad-skin had disappeared into the feast tent and I had gingerly kicked the horrific bottle into the dark grass, I was standing by the tent's entrance, heart banging with excitement.

'Charlie. Could I even go in?

'Could I not?

'I pushed one of the flaps aside with a fingertip and peeped inside. One of those camping gas lights sat on the floor, emitting a strange white-washy light, and I could just about make out Charlie.

'He was sitting on the edge of a little camp bed, his big bare shoulders shiny in the odd light. A blanket was draped over his lap and he was hold-ing his arms awkwardly behind his back. I had to look carefully before I realised, with a surge of lust, that his arms were actually tied behind him.

'He looked up. He looked right at me. Well, at the little sliver of me that must have been visible through the tent flaps, and he said, "Hello, Caro-line." And I was totally shocked that he knew my name.

'"Hi," I said, stepping through the tent entrance. The rain seemed to get harder as I did so, drum-ming urgently on the canvas above me. Not that things like that were really making much impression on me at that moment. My world was so full of Charlie.

'He looked so sexy, sitting there in the half dark, all semi-naked and tied up, that it didn't twig for a moment or two, but then the penny dropped: the odd contrast between Charlie's experience of captivity and my own.

'"How come you're tied up?" I said. "I thought that if you got captured you got to come out of role and just hang out backstage?"

'Charlie snorted. "Because, Caroline, that bastard Tom knows full well that if I wasn't tied up I'd walk straight out of here and up to the game moderators and demand an enquiry into that tricky little fake exchange deal he pulled. It's totally against protocol and he knows it. What's more, tying people up without supervision is pretty dodgy behaviour too. He's going to be in serious trouble the minute I'm out of here. That's why."

'"Oh," I said, "so he's broken the rules?"

'"Yeah," said Charlie, as if I was an idiot. "I'd be surprised if he's allowed to play live combat anywhere in the country when this gets out."

'"Seriously?" That really surprised me. "Well then, why has he done it?"

'"Because, Caroline," Charlie said, very slowly, "he couldn't get his other commanders to agree to a straight swap of me for you. Obviously I'm worth a good deal more than you are, tactically –" he paused dramatically, "– but not to Tom, it would seem."

'I took a few minutes for this to sink in. I couldn't think of anything to say, so I said, "Oh God."

'Charlie shrugged his shoulders. "He does this every so often. Gets a girl he fancies, talks her into playing, gets her done up as a she-orc..." He tailed off into a sigh and then said, "Some of us are more interested in the actual game."

'I looked at the ground for a minute. "So your being here, like this, it's kind of all my fault then."

'"Well, kind of I suppose," said Charlie. "But you can easily make it right. How about you untie me and we both head off to the moderators' camp and sort this mess out."

'And I suppose that would have been the right thing to do, but he looked so sexy all tied up and bristling with his righteous anger. How could I just let him go?

'I moved closer to him, across the tent. "I'll let you go, Charlie, if you do something for me first."

'Charlie looked up at me; I was standing over him at this point and I inched forward, straddling his bare legs.

'He wetted his lips. "What do you want me to do?"

'I didn't answer. There was no need. I bent down and I kissed him. And then I could hear the rain on the roof again, even over the roar of my blood pounding in my ears.

'For a little while he didn't kiss back. He held his mouth still, lips pressed firmly together. I found his reticence strangely arousing, and kept right on working on his mouth, easing and teasing until his lips parted, just a little and his head moved forward a tiny fraction. And he finally gave in and let me kiss him.

'I kissed him for quite a long time, making myself repeat over and over in my head: This is Charlie Baker! You are kissing Charlie Baker! Until I was so wound up and excited I couldn't wait any longer to see his cock.

'I began to work my way downwards. I kissed my way across his throat and down his bare chest. I slipped my hands under the blanket on his lap and found a pair of underpants, barely containing a very hard, very ready cock.

'Charlie inhaled. "Caroline," he said, "I'm not sure if this is a good idea . . ."

'But it was too late. I had just slid his underpants down far enough to liberate his erection. I clapped my right hand over his mouth and smiled up at him. "Now, Charlie, I really don't think that's the kind of thing a barbarian would say."

'And I dipped my head and slid my mouth over his smooth, smooth cock.

'He was hot there. Every other part of his body had been cool, chilled by the cold night air and his lack of clothing. But his cock was hot, so hot that I felt like the contrast was enough to sear my mouth as I sucked. He was delicious.

'When I looked up at him, I saw he had closed his eyes and tipped back his head, with my right hand still clamped over his mouth. His cheeks were gently flushed and his longish hair was drooping across his beautifully sculpted face. I pushed my left hand down between my legs. I wasn't surprised to find that I was very wet.

'Now, although sucking Charlie's cock was all very well – in fact it was a dream come true – I wanted more. I slid my mouth free.

'Charlie's eyes popped open, questioning. I smiled and finally took my hand away from his mouth, looping my arm around his neck instead and pulling him off the camp bed and down on to the groundsheet with me.

'Somehow I managed to get my muddy trousers and knickers off, squirming around Charlie as he knelt on the floor next to me. He looked at my crotch, which was glistening in the pale light. He didn't say anything.

'"I know you want to come, Charlie," I hissed softly, "but I think you should be a proper barbarian gentleman about it and sort me out first." And I stared meaningfully at his beautiful face, before flicking my gaze down.

'Charlie still didn't say anything, but he jerked at his bound wrists. He wanted to be untied first.

'I almost laughed out loud. "Oh no. Not yet, remember? I'm not stupid."

'And with a sigh that I'm sure turned into a smirk, Charlie dipped his head and buried his face between my legs. His tongue touched me almost at once, and I realised how close I was already. I gazed down at him, crouching on the ground with his bound hands poking up in the air, and I found I was bucking up into his mouth. I didn't want a slow build up or anything like that. I'd had enough build up – months of it, in fact! I just wanted Charlie's tongue against my clit right now, over and over until I was coming in his mouth. And in less time than it took to think it, that was what was happening. I clapped my hand over my own mouth then, muffling my cries as I saw tight little blue stars behind my eyes.

'And I didn't forget that I had promised Charlie an orgasm too. In fact, I pulled myself together as quickly as I could, remembering, as my own orgasm faded, that bad-skin had only reckoned on being gone for half an hour. Time was running short.

'I scrambled up into a sitting position and pushed Charlie down on to his back. His cock was harder than ever now, jutting out of his underpants and cherry red. I fell on it, sucking hard, and I couldn't resist working my own clit at the same time, bringing myself back to the peak in a few quick strokes. Charlie jerked hard and desperate as he came, thrusting himself deeper into my mouth, over and over, and his delicious orgasm was enough to make my clit start to spasm all over again – if anything harder and longer than before.

'Not long afterwards, Charlie and I sneaked carefully out of the tent. We raced across the sodden grass and into the woods, where I could see the lights of the barbarian camp not far away.

'"Where's the moderators' camp?" I asked in a whisper. "Aren't they somewhere in the middle?"

'"It's not far."

'We dashed on a little further and then something occurred to me. "Charlie," I hissed.

'"What?"

'"Well, you know that swap thing that Tom pulled? You said it was against protocol or something."

'"Yeah, that's right."

'"Well, surely your team would have reported it to the moderators by now. I mean, they would have noticed pretty quickly that it wasn't you that was handed over."

'Before I'd even finished speaking, Charlie's hand suddenly appeared out of the darkness and grabbed one of my wrists. I tried to jerk it away, but he was far too strong and in a split-second he had tight hold of my other wrist too. Suddenly I was Charlie's prisoner.

'"Oh, Caroline, I'm so sorry," he said in a low voice, "I can't quite believe you fell for that."

'And, ignoring my screams of protest, Charlie whisked me up in the air and flung me over his shoulder. Just moments later I found myself on the damp ground, bathed in the flickering light from the barbarian's camp fire, as all around me Charlie's stunning escape was celebrated with manic whoops and cheers.'

Caroline stops talking. Last orders has come and gone and drinking up is now being urged. Our table is so covered in empty glasses now that there is scarcely room for us to rest our elbows as we all stare at her in awe.

Finally Chris says, 'God, Caroline. That Charlie was a bastard.'

'Not really,' says Caroline, finishing her last vodka tonic, 'he was just bloody good at playing the game.'

'Fuck,' says Mary, who is probably the drunkest of any of us, 'I can't believe you told us all that.'

Caroline laughs. 'Blame that last double you bought me. I was planning to gloss over the explicit stuff a bit more than that, but, well.' And she shrugs as we all stand up and sway our way into our coats.

As we totter out into the night I say, 'So what happened after that, After you were captured again?'

'Oh,' says Caroline, and then smiles a sort of secrety smile, 'I was finally Charlie's prisoner. There were no more exchanges after that.' And she turns and hails a cab, which chugs to a halt at the kerb.

'Was Tom pissed off?'

'Kind of,' she says as she climbs into the warmth, 'but it was only a role play.'

When I get home that night, my husband is sitting at the dining table, painting little miniature goblins with a tiny, tiny brush.

When he hears the door he looks up. 'Hi,' he says, 'good evening?'

'Interesting,' I say, as I slip into the seat opposite him and glance at the fantastical army spread across the table top.

'Good,' he says, going back to his painting.

I purse my lips and watch him for a minute. Then I say, 'Charlie, you went to Sheffield University, right? Ever meet a girl called Caroline?'

Violet Parker's short story, *Greek God*, appears in the Wicked Words collection *Sex at the Sports Club*.